RIVERBOY

Illustrated by
Jim Marsh

RIVERBOY

Billy C. Clark

Edited by
Tracey Besmark

The Jesse Stuart Foundation
Ashland, KY
1997

To my wife Ruth, my son Billy,
my daughter Melissa, and
my three grandchildren Benjamin,
Timothy, and Jodi Elizabeth.

Riverboy

Library of Congress Cataloging-in-Publication Data

Clark, Billy C. (Billy Curtis)
    Riverboy / Billy C. Clark ; edited by Tracey Besmark.
        p.   cm.
    ISBN 0-945084-65-X
    I. Besmark, Tracey, 1966- . II. Title.
PS3505.L2425R58 1997   97-25377
813' .54--dc21   CIP

Published by:
The Jesse Stuart Foundation
P.O. Box 391
Ashland, KY 41114
1997

Introduction

On March 4 of this year (1997), the floodgates were closed on the floodwall built around my hometown of Catlettsburg, Kentucky. The floodgates were closed to hold back the rising waters of the Ohio and Big Sandy Rivers. Predictions were that the two rivers would rise above floodstage of 53 feet, and those predictions proved to be right when the rivers finally reached a crest of 59 feet, 8 inches. The floodwall saved the town from yet another flooding.

When word reached me of the impendent flood, two things came quickly to mind. My first thought was of the timeliness of my novel *Riverboy*, a book about the building of the floodwall around Catlettsburg and of the change it brought to a young riverboy and an old man who lived along the banks of the rivers. My second thoughts were nostalgic. If I had been there, I could have predicted what the rivers would or would not do by reading their signs. As a boy, I had learned the two rivers that well. The rivers were my home; they still are and will be forever. But also among my thoughts was the knowledge that predicting was one thing; preventing the rivers from swelling over into the town was another. The floodwall kept that from happening.

I grew up along the rivers prior to the building of the floodwall, or, as old timers there used to say: "before the wall of concrete and earth stole the rivers from the town." And so I have been privileged to know the rivers before and after--before, when the two rivers could be seen from almost anywhere in town, and after they had been "stolen away." I have vivid memories of many floods, beginning with the legendary and treacherous flood of 1937. By the age of ten, I had oared a johnboat up and down most of the streets of the little river town of Catlettsburg and over the tops of many of its buildings. I rescued people who had misjudged the rivers and chose to "ride them out." They ended up holding on to the tops of buildings, fighting the current until I could take them to high grounds, which were the hills a short distance away.

During my growing up years, Catlettsburg was a land of great beauty. During quieter times, the water of the two rivers was as blue as a Robin's egg. Cotton bloom willows grew up their banks to the edge of a hand-laid brick road at the edge of town, a road known appropriately as Front Street. In the summer, the riverwind carried the white cotton blooms of the willows over the streets of town. Silent as a hush, they fell like puffs of cotton. The song of the birds living along the rivers could be heard across town where the level narrow strip of land shouldered the rugged hills harrowing the clouds.

The old weather-whipped, lizard-grey rock that measured floodstage for the town had been embedded in the earth longer than anyone could remember. From there, in the center of the brick road, I could watch the great paddlewheels churn the water as they pushed tow up the mighty Ohio, from near the center during normal tide and "hugging the willows for easy water" when the river was "up a mite" and the current was strong. From there, I stood in Kentucky and looked across the Big Sandy at West Virginia, the state coming to a point and ending at the mouth of the Big Sandy, and then I glanced across the Ohio to see the state of Ohio. Old rivermen tied their shantyboats to many willows hugging the rivers edge, and the banks held driftwood cabins of those who chose to live on land. Indeed, the land and the two rivers inspired my storytelling, for it was an exciting place to grow up.

The floodwall brought change to Catlettsburg and to the two rivers that framed the town. That change is what *Riverboy* is all about: a riverboy and an old man who claimed the rivers as their home.

Billy C. Clark

Chapter 1

Brad stood outside his house waiting for his mother. From there, he could see all the way across the small town of Catlettsburg. If he squinted his eyes from the sun, he could see where the end of the town dipped and slid into the waters of the Big Sandy River near the cabin of Dan Tackett.

It was growing late. The sun had risen high enough to peek over the tops of the hills behind Brad's house. By now, Brad knew, the warm rays of the sun would have reached the river and would be doing strange things to the smooth surface of the water. At this time of year the water would be smooth and lazy, and the bright sun would be changing it to many colors. The water resembled, as Dan Tackett had once told him, a large rainbow that had grown tired of bending across the sky and had stretched out on its side among the hills of Eastern Kentucky to rest during the heat of the day.

Brad began to grow tired and restless from waiting. His mother had told him that she had some business to take care of in town, and she promised to walk part way with him to Dan Tackett's cabin. He wished she would hurry.

Dan Tackett lived in a small cabin that sat low on the banks of the river near the hum of the current. From his front porch, on a night when the moon was bright, you could sit with your arms folded and watch the smooth water drift in and out under the shadows of the willows that hugged the edge of the shore. There was a large sand bar in the center of the narrow river. Under the light of the moon, the white sand was as bright as the bark of the water birch where the sand bar broke the smooth surface of the water. From the cabin you could watch the small ripples form as the water washed over the sand—ripples drifting over shallow water, wrinkling toward the cabin until they disappeared under the willows.

The cabin sat on the Kentucky shore. Across the river rose the West Virginia Point, cutting the river like the point of a spear. Down river the Big Sandy emptied into the broad Ohio. The Big Sandy was not a wide river. Dan Tackett claimed he had once sailed a rock across it when he was younger. Still, it was a beautiful river.

This time of year the cabin would be shaded by the long slender leaves of the willows. One great willow stood almost within arm's reach of the old man's cabin; within its boughs Cindy, a catbird that Dan Tackett had named, would be building her nest again this year.

The cabin was not far enough over the bank to be hidden from town. At the cabin, Brad could stand on his tiptoes and look over the narrow streets of the town. In fact, the very cabin itself stood on unused town property. The old man had built his cabin there many years ago and had always lived in it rent free. No one in the town had ever objected; the old man always seemed to be a part of the town itself.

Brad did not know how long Dan had lived there. But it seemed that Dan Tackett had forever earned his living from the fish he took from the river and from tending his small gardens along the shore. Many people in Catlettsburg said that Dan Tackett was as old as the willow that grew beside his cabin. Others said that he was so old that he had become part of the river. And like the waters of the Big Sandy, they figured he would drift along always.

Dan Tackett had surely lived long enough to become part of the river. Brad thought that Dan had lived long enough to know more about the river than the river knew of itself.

The Big Sandy was usually a quiet, lazy river, but it could also be a moody river. And being moody, there were times when it grew angry. Fed by mountain streams, the river would grow angry enough to swell over the banks, flooding the small town of Catlettsburg, and driving people from their homes. And when the river's anger ceased, the town would be left with a cover of black river mud that had to be scraped from the homes and streets and carried back to the river. It was during the river's anger that Dan Tackett came to help the town. Because he knew the river so well, the old man always knew when the anger would come. Throughout the months of February and March, the old man would watch the river creep inch by inch up the bank toward town. During the night while the town slept, he would travel to the edge of the water and shove a willow stick into the ground where the water had reached. At night, while the town slept, the old man would travel back and forth gauging how far the water had risen upon the stick. He would stand in the darkness and study the signs of the sky to see if more rain would come to swell the river higher. He would judge the current that he knew could take the bulge out of the stream; then, pulling his stick and swinging it back and forth to dry it in the wind, he would shove it in the ground farther up the bank, following the rising water.

Dan Tackett was happy when he was matching his wits against the river. If he gave the word, the town would come alive. If he said the river would soon burst over its banks, the townspeople gathered their belongings and moved them safely to higher ground. Anchoring his small cabin to the giant willow with ropes and wire, the old man would gather his meager belongings in sacks and walk quickly to town where he supervised the tying of other homes and buildings that might be carried away by the strong current.

When the river had risen just as Dan Tackett had predicted, it was the old man who untied his joeboat from the willows and paddled up and down the streets of town, helping those who had been late getting to high ground, and carrying news to people about their abandoned homes.

Nobody remembered when Dan Tackett began watching the river for the town. It just seemed to be something that had happened. In judging the river, the old man was always right. There had been times, of course, when many had doubted him. Sometimes they would doubt when the river crept within inches of the top of the bank, but Dan Tackett would stand at the water's edge, grinning at it.

"Reckon the river is plenty mad," he would say, "but its anger is about gone. Tomorrow the river will go down. It will come no higher."

And still there were some who sneaked off, carrying their furniture and belongings away from the river. And the old man would watch them the next day as they carried their belongings back home.

Some people tried to outwit the river themselves. They would not leave their homes. These were the people the old man paddled away in his joeboat when the water flooded the town.

Dan Tackett was part of the river sure enough, Brad thought. And he was also part of the town. The town loved him and respected him. What a great world Dan Tackett owns, Brad thought. His impatience returning, Brad looked toward the door again to see if his mother was coming. Although it might not seem so much different from the other days of the week, this day had a special meaning for Brad, and it made him fret to delay. This was the first day of May, and it had been special since the first time Brad had traveled to the cabin of Dan Tackett. This was the day each year that Captain Bozer and his tugboat *Chatterwa* came nosing up the Big Sandy to begin summer trading. Brad felt that he and Dan Tackett had to be on hand to greet Dan Tackett's great friend Captain Bozer. It just wouldn't be right at all to miss him.

Why was it taking his mother so long? He grew more anxious. This year it seemed more important than ever to be with Dan Tackett when Captain Bozer came upriver. This summer looked the same as other summers, yet it was different somehow. This year there was talk in town of something called a flood wall. And in some strange way the flood wall was connected with Dan Tackett.

Brad had first learned of this flood wall shortly after his mother had begun attending meetings held in the small town hall. Later people gathered in different houses in town. One night they had gathered in Brad's home. Brad had gone to bed but had not fallen asleep. The name of Dan Tackett had been mentioned. Next came talk of the flood wall. The flood wall was to be built around the town, a wall high enough to hold out the river when it became angry. Brad could not hear all that was said, but he heard the name Dan Tackett again and again.

Then, very soon after, Brad had been asked to stay at the home of a neighbor while his mother traveled with a group from the town all the way to the Capitol where the President lived. And here, Brad learned, they had talked again of the wall. When his mother had returned, she had talked of their need for a flood wall to hold out the river, and the President had promised enough money to build it. Soon an engineer would be coming to begin the wall. It would be built by pushing dirt from the banks of the river into a great heap along the rim of the town. With the engineer would come trucks and bulldozers to shove dirt so high the river could not climb it.

Brad's first thought was for Dan Tackett. What would the old man do if he was shoved from the river and the ground that he gardened along the river bank?

"But if the dirt is pushed from the river bank," Brad had said, tears welling in his eyes, "will they push Dan Tackett away?"

Brad's mother had stared at him for a long time.

"The wall will not harm Dan Tackett," she said. She told Brad once again how the river was forever eating away at the town of Catlettsburg. The town was slowly disappearing and many people were moving down river to towns untouched by high water. People did not want to live where water was apt to wash muck and mud into their homes each year, bringing disease and sometimes death with it.

"But Dan Tackett will let them know when the river is coming," Brad said.

"I know," his mother answered. "Dan Tackett is a wonderful person. But even Dan Tackett cannot stop the river from coming. The whole world is growing, Brad, but Catlettsburg is disappearing. Our town will grow too, with the flood wall."

"But why must we grow?" Brad asked. "I like Catlettsburg just the way it is. And so does Dan Tackett."

"Try to understand, Brad," his mother said, frowning. "Dan Tackett is an old man. He lives in an old world. Dan Tackett will become a part of our new world, when the flood wall comes. It is a wonderful thing. You'll see. And so will Dan Tackett, I am sure." His mother rubbed her hands through her hair. "Now don't you worry. No harm will come to Dan Tackett."

"I don't care if the flood wall never comes," Brad said.

"Now wait and see," his mother answered. "Since your father died, I have always tried to teach you one thing: Before you make up your mind about anything, you must think about it. Think hard about it. Often you will have a different answer from your first thought. The flood wall is no different. You must think about it."

Brad had thought about the flood wall. He had lain in bed nights and tried to picture the great wall his mother spoke about, but his answer was always the same. He had seen the flood wall always as a dark shadow at the edge of the town shutting out the river, shutting out Dan Tackett's cabin. He remembered the words of his mother. His world was one of progress and machines. But he knew his mother was wrong. His world was one of trees, hills, and the Big Sandy River without a wall bordering it. And Dan Tackett would be in his world to watch over the river. Perhaps, he

17

thought, his mother was wrong about the flood wall. It had not come to Catlettsburg yet. And to Dan Tackett's way of thinking, it would not come at all. Dan Tackett had not spoken much of it.

"It is a foolish notion, Brad," he said. "Like high water, it will come and go."

Brad shook away notions of the flood wall and turned his head to gauge the sun. He would have to hurry today. He knew that his mother would walk slowly. It was almost time. And Dan Tackett would be waiting.

"Hurry, Ma," he said, as his mother walked out of the house. "You'll cause me to miss the *Chatterwa* and Captain Bozer when they nose into the Big Sandy. An' Captain Bozer would sure be sad on his trip up the river."

"Not nearly as sad as you," his mother said, grinning.

This time his mother was right, Brad thought, as they looked toward town. He would be the saddest of all. As sure as the river would rise this time of year, Captain Bozer would be upriver today. The channel of the river would be deeper now and Captain Bozer would come to travel the length of the Big Sandy selling store goods or trading them to towns along the shore for herbs and furs.

For many years Captain Bozer had pulled the tug to shore at the river's mouth to give a long toot of his whistle for Dan Tackett.

Then Brad would come, sit on the porch of the cabin, and watch and wave with Dan Tackett. And last year there had come a long toot of the whistle and then a short one. The short whistle had been for Brad. Dan Tackett had said that Brad was surely a riverman now. And in the days that followed Brad had strained his eyes to watch for the little tug to come back down the river.

It was hard for Brad to walk as slowly as his mother. Several times he had to stop and wait for her. Finally she stopped and spoke to Brad.

"You must be home before dark," she said.

Brad watched his mother as she walked slowly toward the town hall. There would be another meeting about the flood wall today, he thought, strangely troubled. He stared for a minute. Then he took a deep breath and turned toward the river and the quiet world of Dan Tackett.

Chapter 2

If Brad had walked straight toward the river, he would have reached the river bank directly above the cabin of Dan Tackett. Instead, he turned down the main street of the town and walked for nearly a block before he turned toward the river. Now that he was close to the river and the cabin of the old man, he was less worried about missing Captain Bozer. From the path he could hear the putt-putt of the motor on the little tug, and he was sure that he could reach the cabin ahead of it.

Brad thought of the little tug, and of Captain Bozer. And he thought of the name *Chatterwa* that Captain Bozer had given the little tug. Once Dan Tackett had told him that he figured Captain Bozer had taken the name from the Chatterwaha, which was the name given to the Big Sandy River by the Indians, meaning "river of many sand bars." And yet Captain Bozer had laughed and said the name had come after he had put a motor on the back of the tug. The putt-putt of the motor seemed to be always chattering at the river. Before the motor was added to the tug, Captain Bozer had poled the boat upriver. He had lived on this tug for a long time. He had not been fast in accepting a motor.

For Captain Bozer, like Dan Tackett, lived in a slow-moving world of the river. But the swift currents of the river and old age had forced him to modernize the tug or give it up altogether. And Captain Bozer was a riverman.

On this trip, Captain Bozer would gain knowledge from Dan Tackett of the river since he had last traveled it. Here at the river's mouth, the sand bar that broke the surface was hard to judge. The changing current of the river played tricks with it, carrying sand and dropping it along the edges of the bar, building it up and spreading it out. The more the bar spread, the more shallow the river became, yet much of the sand was not piled high enough to break the surface of the water.

Only one thing was certain: The channel of the river hugged the Kentucky shore. Yet, here was danger, too. Along the edges of the bank, snags of giant willows that had long ago lost their tops to the swift current lay hidden under the surface of the water. To make matters worse, these hazards changed each year. Only Dan Tackett would know what the river was up to. He would know how wide the channel was and where it ran deepest. He would know how far the sand bar had crept underwater toward the Kentucky shore. And he would also know which snags still remained along the edges of the bank. He would know how far out in the water the small tug must remain.

He did not have to measure the depth of the water along the edge of the sand bar. He had been with the river too long to be fooled by it. He had only to stick his hand into the water and judge the current of the river. From the force of the water, he could judge the amount of silt it carried. If the water was heavy, he knew that the sand bar had crept much closer to the Kentucky shore. This meant that Captain Bozer must hold much closer to the Kentucky shore—just far enough out in the river to miss the snags. But if the river was calm with only a slow current, the water would be deeper even close to the edge of the sand bar. This way the Captain would not have to worry. There would be a clear, wide channel.

Captain Bozer went up the river on the West Virginia side, putting in at all the towns along the way. And then, making his turn, he would drift back down the Kentucky side, making his stops there too. He would stop along the shore until there was no light left, and then he would drift out of the Big Sandy after dark. There were many times when he passed the cabin of Dan Tackett under a heavy fog after dark.

Dan Tackett not only allowed for the sand bar, but knew what night Captain Bozer would drift out of the river. And if Dan Tackett judged it to be a night of fog, he always provided a way so that his great friend would not run aground in the little tug. He hung a lantern on one of the branches of the giant willow that stood beside his cabin. If the lantern was lit, it could be seen even through the heaviest fog for a long distance upriver. The light from the lantern would be a sign that the sand bar had built and spread. Captain Bozer would know he had to steer the tug closer to the Kentucky shore. If there was no light in the lantern, then Captain Bozer would know that the channel was wide and he could stay much farther out in the river.

Brad thought of the tug as he stepped onto the path and started upriver. He thought of the old man, Dan Tackett.

Then he stopped for a moment and wondered about the flood wall his mother had spoken of. He imagined the great wall being so high that it could hold out the river. This alone, he thought, would not be such a bad thing. But the wall would be built of earth, scooped from the banks of the river where it would be close at hand. This would mean that the great willows that shaded the river would be scraped from their home. What would happen to Dan Tackett?

He thought of the trucks and bulldozers that would push up the earth. One had passed through town not so long ago. It had gone to the upper end of the town where work would soon begin on the flood wall. He could not keep the chills from going over his body when he thought of the truck. It had been bigger than the cabin where Dan Tackett lived. In the front seat of the truck had sat the driver, with another man beside him. The passenger was waving his hand back and forth, pointing toward the river. This man had caught Brad staring at the truck and had grinned and waved at him. Brad had only stared. He had not waved back. Dan Tackett would not have waved either, he had thought. Yet the man had had a friendly face. But sometimes, Brad thought, the looks of a man could be deceiving, as the river was at times. One day the river could be so lazy that you could hardly hear it wash against the banks. And just when you were ready to believe it could be trusted, it would swell and drive with angry force across the streets of town, destroying as it went.

Perhaps that was the way of the stranger. At any rate Brad had not waved.

These men in the truck were not of the same world as Dan Tackett. And neither were they from Brad's world. Brad knew that this was his world, here along the path that led to Dan Tackett's cabin.

Brad shook the notion of the flood wall from his mind and thought instead of the river-world around him. If this was to be his home, he must learn it. Here under the shade of the willow, birch, and maple were many secrets that could not be learned in a book. In fact, Dan Tackett had told him that there were many things here he would never be able to learn.

Ever since the first mention of the flood wall, Brad had grown closer to the old man; he felt that he must learn the river this summer, or be caught in a whirlpool of a changing world. A world his mother called progress. A world of machines and flood walls.

Brad watched a catbird sail over the tops of the trees. He followed the bird with his eyes until it lighted on the top of a birch, fluffed its feathers, and then glided out of sight. He had watched the birds along the river for a long time. He had learned to mock the catcall of the gray catbird so well that he could often persuade the bird to answer his call. And yet the catbird and its language were strange to him. He knew that he did not belong completely to the world of Dan Tackett. He had not been with the river long enough.

Brad started upriver, then suddenly he stopped again. A chunk of clay tumbled down from a spot where the bank was steep and bare. He squatted and turned to face the steep bank. His eyes rested on a small hole that had been dug in the side of the bank and a smile came to his face. A kingfisher slowly stuck its head from the hole and looked all around as if it were trying to find

Brad squatted beneath the willows. The bird stared, turning its head from side to side. And then it flew quickly out of the hole and into the trees and was lost from sight. The bird would be back, Brad thought, as he straightened up. The hole in the steep bank was its nest. The kingfisher, he thought, had gone to the sand bar to search for a minnow. Brad knew that the dried leaves and grass the kingfisher had carried there in her bill were tucked inside the bank. And this time of year there were apt to be eggs in the nest.

The kingfisher knew the river. It was one of the smartest of all birds, according to Dan Tackett. It did not build its nest in a tree where wild animals, humans, or even a heavy wind might destroy it. Not even a snake, which loved to rob the nests of birds, could hold to the side of the steep bank. From high up the bank the kingfisher could spot an enemy a long distance away and peek from the hole above until the danger was gone.

Brad wondered if the kingfisher was smart enough to know how lucky she was, being able to live so close to the river all the time. She could sit at the mouth of the hole at night and watch the moon sparkle on the water and listen to the hum of the river. How good it would be to be sung to sleep at night by the lazy sounds of the winds through the leaves of the willows.

Just then, a sound drifted through the willows. Brad

cocked his ears. The muffled putt-putt came again. Captain Bozer, he thought, and his heart beat fast. He must race now to beat the boat to the cabin. Dan Tackett would be waiting. He ran up the path, dodging the willow saplings that hovered over the path.

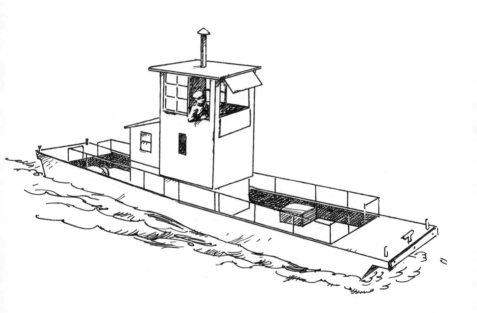

Chapter 3

Getting closer to the cabin, Brad stopped to catch his breath. Dan Tackett would think he was not coming today. He would sneak into the yard and surprise him.

Near the edge of the yard, Brad looked toward the small cabin. The old man sat in the chair on the front porch, his hands folded across his lap. His head was cocked toward the river, and Brad knew that Dan Tackett too had heard the sound of the tug. Brad walked a little closer until he was by the side of the giant willow. He leaned against the tree and took a deep breath.

"He's coming, Dan Tackett!" Brad hollered. "Listen!"

"By-doggies!" Dan Tackett said, looking toward Brad with a great smile on his face. "I'll say he is for sure."

Dan Tackett stood and dusted his hands on the faded overalls he wore.

"Come might near beating you upriver this time, didn't he?" the old man said. "Didn't think you was going to make it today."

Dan Tackett stretched his back. But as hard as he stretched he could not straighten it all the way. His back was bent with age, like an old willow. Once, when Brad

had been too young to know that he should not have asked such a question, he had asked the old man why his back was so bowed. Dan Tackett had laughed at him. "I suppose it is maybe like that tree there." He pointed his finger at an old willow, bent so low that its top reached the sand. "There is no sap left in the roots to bring new life," he had said.

A light wind swept behind Brad and the old man as they walked up the path. Dan Tackett lifted his hand and brushed it back over his head.

"It would have been shorter to have come straight across town and down over the edge of the bank," Dan Tackett said.

"How . . . how . . . did you know I came up the river path?" Brad asked.

"Come here, Brad," he said, placing his hand on Brad's shoulder as Brad walked closer. "Look through there." He pointed his finger through the low branches of the willows. "Now, tell me what you see."

Following the finger of the old man, Brad squinted his eyes and looked at the tip of the sand bar. There was something moving on the end of it. Brad looked up at Dan Tack/ett.

"It's a kingfisher," he said.

"And what is it doing?" Dan Tackett asked.

Brad watched the bird closely.

"Nothing," he said. "It's just standing there on the edge of the bar."

"Not searching for a minnow?" Dan Tackett asked.

Brad looked again. The bird stood motionless.

"Nope," Brad said. "Just standing there looking."

"Which way is it looking?" the old man asked.

Brad looked harder through the trees.

"She . . . she is looking toward the bank," Brad said.

"Well, now," Dan Tackett said, rubbing his chin, "I wonder why she would be staring toward the bank. She ought to be searching the edge of the sand bar for a minnow. That's what she usually goes there for. She shouldn't be staring back at the bank at all. That is"—the old man rubbed his chin harder—"unless someone scared her along the river bank. Maybe someone who had stopped along the path to stare at the nest where she had hid her eggs. And then maybe she flew through the trees to lead them away. Maybe she flew over the cabin of Dan Tackett in a hurry. And maybe she is standing there afraid to go back. Afraid she will lead someone back to her nest."

Brad kicked at the earth under his feet.

"Oh shucks, Dan Tackett," he said. "I didn't fool you at all. You knew I was coming up the path all the time didn't you?"

"Well, now, Brad," Dan Tackett said, "you oughten to

feel too bad. It ain't easy to fool an old riverman. Now you take that river out there"—Dan Tackett made a wide sweep with his hand—"look how long it has been trying to fool Dan Tackett. Ain't done it yet though." A smile came to the old man's face. "And one day maybe the river won't be fooling you either. One day when old Dan Tackett has left the river the cabin might well be yours. And then this river will be yours, and you will have to know it just as I do now."

"But I don't reckon you will ever leave it," Brad said, smiling at the old man. "And I would much rather the river be mine and yours together."

Dan Tackett looked upriver for a minute. And then he looked back at Brad. There was a frown on his face. In fact, there was a look on it that Brad had never seen before.

"Maybe not for a little while," Dan Tackett said. "I reckon not as long as the town wants me."

"But the town will always want you to watch the river," Brad said. "The river will always grow angry and swell over the banks. You told me so yourself."

"That I did," Dan Tackett said. "But maybe time can change a lot of things." He looked upriver again. "The town is growing fast. I can remember when you could count the buildings in the town on your fingers. Now look at it. Buildings are everywhere. The first buildings were made of logs that were floated down this river and drug up the bank. They were built by hand. Now they can set a building up with a machine. Why, maybe one day the eyes of an old man will be replaced by some sort of a machine. This will be a different world than the one I know. I believe folks call it progress." The old man shook his head. "And it just might be this world is not too far up the river."

Tears welled in Brad's eyes as he watched the old man. He hated the truck that he had watched on the street in town. No machine could ever take the place of Dan Tackett, he thought, no matter how big it was.

Abruptly, the quiet of the river was broken by the long blast of a whistle.

The first blast of the whistle drifted through the trees and ended. And the river again became so quiet that Brad knew for sure Dan Tackett could hear his heart beat. And then it came again. This time it was a short blast of the whistle. And Brad knew that it was the prettiest sound he had ever heard. The short blast was meant for him. It was a sure sign that Captain Bozer knew that Brad was also at the cabin. The whistle seemed to say: You are sure enough a riverman too.

Dan Tackett grinned and patted Brad on the shoulder.

"We had best be going to the edge of the river," he

said, brushing his hair once again from his face. "Captain Bozer is pulling toward shore."

Chapter 4

Brad followed the old man down the path to the edge of the river. Stepping to the side of a short, bushy willow, he looked out over the water. The small tug had turned and nosed toward the bank. Already the first waves from the boat reached the shore. And the small joeboat that Dan Tackett kept locked to a willow bobbled up and down against the waves.

Slowly Captain Bozer pulled the tug to the shore, standing at the front of the small deck. His hair blew in the wind that came off the river, and he stood, one foot propped on the edge of the railing that framed the deck of the small tug. Captain Bozer was the largest man that Brad had ever seen. While he moved around on the deck of the small tug as if his feet were as light as those of a catbird, his enormous body seemed as if it would surely turn the little boat over should he lean over the railing. His hair was red, a red as deep in color as the red bricks that formed the old buildings along the rim of the town. Yet the red somehow was much shinier. The sun seemed to sparkle from it, and the river wind blew it as freely as if it were the top of a small sapling.

Captain Bozer pulled the boat closer to the shore

and threw a short line toward Dan Tackett. Dan Tackett grabbed the line, made a quick twist around a willow tree with it, and held the loose end.

"How be you, Dan Tackett?" Captain Bozer said, reaching his large hand over the side of the boat.

Dan Tackett stretched over the water until his hand reached Captain Bozer's.

"Reckon I am all right," he said.

Captain Bozer looked away from Dan Tackett and stared at Brad with his deep-set eyes.

"Hop in the joeboat, Brad," he said, "so you can shake hands."

Brad stepped into the joeboat, walked carefully to the back seat and stretched until he could touch the side of the tug. He felt the grip of Captain Bozer's hand and then his feet flew out from under him. He was lifted through the air like a bird and set down on the deck. "By-doggie, Dan Tackett," Captain Bozer said, "if it weren't for my needing another set of eyes here to watch the sand bar, I'd be apt to take this riverman from you. I'll bet his eyes are as keen to the river as yours."

Captain Bozer glanced down at the surface of the water and stared at it, rubbing his chin.

"Speaking of the river," he said, looking at Dan Tackett, "ain't the river carrying a lot of mud and sand for this time of year?"

Dan Tackett stared at the river. "Ain't natural," he said. "But this mud and sand ain't got anything to do with the flow of the water. You will pass it once you are a piece upriver."

"Well now, Dan Tackett," Captain Bozer said. "There must be something that's mighty unnatural. The river don't carry mud and sand without a reason."

"The river, I reckon, is having dirt pushed into it," Dan Tackett said.

"And what is pushing it?" Captain Bozer said, leaning farther over the edge of the tug.

"Reckon," Dan Tackett said, brushing his hair away from his face, "people in Catlettsburg have got the foolish notion about a flood wall. Planning to keep this river out of the town, they think. Ain't been a word said to me about it, but I ain't fooled. I been watching their trucks and bulldozers go through town. I may be an old man, but I ain't fooled. And I ain't catering to none of this foolishness. I wash my hands right now of the whole foolish notion. There ain't no trucks or bulldozers or anything going to keep this river back." Dan Tackett drew up his lower lip and frowned. "Progress they call it. Did they ask for the word of Dan Tackett about the river like they always have before? No. A ruination, I would have told them. They knew it too. Well, they've needed the word of Dan Tackett about the river before, and they'll need it again."

Captain Bozer eyed upriver and rubbed his chin again. But he could not see far. A bend in the river hid the upper end of the small town from sight. He studied for a minute and then grinned at Dan Tackett.

"'Pon-my-word," he said, slapping the side of his leg again, "what's the matter, Dan Tackett? You ain't fell asleep and let this river sneak up on them, have you?"

A frown came to Brad's face. He wished for once that Captain Bozer would not joke like this. But Brad had never remembered Dan Tackett getting upset over it. This time was no different.

"Ain't fell asleep yet," Dan Tackett said. "But" — he rubbed his own chin — "maybe I might before long. Could be it would be just when you would be coming back down the river. Say . . . on a foggy night. If I should happen to fall asleep, I wouldn't be able to light the lantern." He grinned for the first time since he had reached the edge of the river.

Captain Bozer studied the water for a minute, still rubbing his chin. Then he looked this time at Brad and grinned.

"I reckon I would have to depend on Brad then," he said. "He would have to light the lantern for me."

Brad's face turned red again.

"I reckon Brad would," Dan Tackett said. "Reckon

from the way things stand, Brad is about the only friend I got left that I can depend on. Some people are fast to forget old Dan Tackett. But not Brad."

Brad's chest swelled with pride.

Captain Bozer looked at Brad.

"Well," he said, "I can see right now that I will have to bargain with you both or not bargain at all." He glanced at Dan Tackett. "Pay no attention to them, Dan Tackett. Towns all along this river here have been talking about flood walls since the day I was big enough to pull a joeboat across the river, and nothing has ever come of most of it. Trucks and bulldozers move in and push up a little dirt here and there and the river raises on them and washes it away, dirt, notions, and all. They'll depend on you again, just like I do."

Dan Tackett stared at the little tug.

"How is the *Chatterwa* holding up these days?"

"Still the best boat on either river," Captain Bozer said. "Big Sandy or Ohio." He took a deep breath and patted the railing around the deck. "Just like the day she was built. Got several years under her keel, but just like a Big Sandy woman, she don't show her age at all."

Captain Bozer continued: "Now, here's something for you. You talk about the flood-wall notion. It ain't only flood walls; it's boats too. People on down the Ohio River all laugh at the *Chatterwa*. 'Why don't you get yourself a boat, Captain Bozer?' they say. 'That chunk of driftwood you're a-floating is about twenty years behind the times.' And then they point out some new boat that looks like it was built to put in a picture frame and say: 'Now there's a boat for you. One trip on a boat like that up the Big Sandy River and you can haul back more roots and herbs and hides than you could haul in a summer in that tug. This is a different world now, Bozer,' they will say. Then they will speak of progress." Captain Bozer grinned and patted the railing of the *Chatterwa* again. "They ain't about to fool me with their progress, though. I look at their new boat and I say that I have seen boats made from driftwood timber that would take the water better. No sir. There ain't but one boat for me. The *Chatterwa* and me are happy just as we are. And we aim to stay that way. That is, unless you were not just kidding about letting the lantern go out."

"Well," Dan Tackett said, "don't reckon I will have to worry about the lantern going out at all if you intend to dock here permanent. The raise will be over this month and the river will come out swift. If you intend to stand here and talk until you won't be needing me to light the lantern at all."

"I was just thinking along the same line," Captain Bozer said. "I was thinking that if you didn't unwind my rope from that willow tree it would be apt to grow

41

to the side of it."

With this Dan Tackett took the hitch out of the rope and threw it toward the deck of the tug. Captain Bozer grabbed the end of the rope and quickly rolled it in a coil on the deck. Brad climbed over the side of the tug and stepped into the joeboat. Then he walked along the bottom of the boat onto the bank, and he stood beside the old man.

Captain Bozer looked at Brad and grinned.

"Watch the old man, Brad. Be sure that he don't fall asleep," he said.

Dan Tackett quickly stooped, rose, and hurled a handful of sand toward the tug.

"Be on upriver with you," he said, as the small grains of sand pelleted the surface of the water. "The lantern will be lit." He raised his hand as the *Chatterwa* nosed upriver, cutting the water.

Dan Tackett stared at the small tug longer than usual. He blinked his eyes from the sun and stood with his hands on his hips. Then he glanced at a still pool of water cradled between the roots of a big willow.

A light film of muddy water seeped past the roots and mixed in the pool, hiding the bottom. Dan Tackett looked upriver and shook his head. A frown was on his face. And from upriver came the sound of a motor of a truck. Next came the grinding sound of a bulldozer.

Chapter 5

Dan Tackett frowned as he sat on the porch of his cabin and stared into the limbs of the giant willow that stood in the yard.

The giant willow too, Brad thought, showed signs of age. In places along the huge trunk the bark had peeled and the old flesh of the tree had turned brown against the sun. On some of the limbs, the small green leaves blew in the warm summer wind. But on other limbs the leaves would never grow again. They were old, brown, and bowed—here and there along the lower limbs, pieces of brush—old leaves carried by years of high water—were glued to the bark by the river mud. The tree had stood many years struggling with the soft earth of sand and black loam trying to bed its roots deeper. It had stood against the current of the river when it rose in anger. It was surely a tough old tree, stubborn as the river itself, Dan Tackett had once told Brad. In a fork near the top of the tree, was the home of the catbird named Cindy.

The catbird had returned for the last two summers to the nest in the giant willow to hatch her eggs. She still eyed Dan Tackett as he moved around under her nest, but she would fly low in his yard to gather bread crumbs that he threw there for her. She had learned to trust the old man.

Cindy watched Dan Tackett as he sat down in his chair. She moved around patching her nest that had almost been destroyed by high water since she had hatched her brood there last summer.

The old man looked again upriver from where the purr of the motors came. He rubbed his hands together and shook his head.

"Do you reckon . . ." Brad said, and then stopped.

Dan Tackett looked quickly at him.

"Do you reckon," Brad continued, "that the flood wall will really come?" He glanced toward the ground, sorry in a way that he had mentioned the flood wall to Dan Tackett, and yet anxious to know the opinion of the old man.

"Maybe," Dan Tackett said. "Can't really tell yet, Brad."

Brad frowned upriver.

"Let them build their flood wall," Brad said, pushing his lower lip over his upper. "They can't hurt you with it, can they, Dan Tackett?"

"Don't reckon I rightly know," Dan Tackett said, still rubbing his hands. "But from what little I hear of it, the flood wall will be built on top of the river bank. They will need a lot of dirt from the banks of the river. I figure if they get down river this far they ought to about be where my cabin sets."

Brad felt a chill at the old man's words.

"What will you do, Dan Tackett?" Brad asked.

"Don't know," the old man said. "It just don't seem right that the town would want to take my home from me. If they did, I just don't reckon I would know what to do. Ain't ever done nothing but live here watching the river." He glanced at Brad. Brad had puckered his lip higher. And a smile came to the face of the old man. "Now don't you go to fretting about anything, Brad. Ain't nothing going to happen to Dan Tackett. I have lived here with the town and the river too long to be pushed off by a bunch of city slickers and their modern trucks and bulldozers. This might be what they call a world of progress, but in my world I have learned a few tricks. When the time comes, I will show them what good their flood wall really is. Right now, though, it looks like me and you have got to stick together."

Brad grinned and he eyed the old man with pride.

"Where will we start, Dan Tackett?" Brad asked, anxious to begin.

"Well now, Brad," Dan Tackett said, "I think I know the place. We will start with this flood wall just like I started with this river years ago. And just like you are starting with it now. We will start at the beginning. We will use our keen eyes and ears and observe what is going on around us."

Brad stared at the old man as if he were not sure he understood what had been said. And Dan Tackett looked at him and grinned.

"It ought to work, Brad," he said. "It did for me. I learned the river. Now there are people in town who will say that old Dan Tackett has some magic powers that he uses to know when the river is coming up over the banks. This is a foolish notion; the only magic power I have ever used is the magic the good Lord gave in my eyes and ears."

Dan Tackett stretched his back in the chair and squinted his eyes. "When I first came to know this river, Brad, I was no bigger than you are now. And at first the river fooled me bad. I did not know the many reasons why the river came over the bank. Yet I tried mighty hard to judge it. I reckon back at that time I thought there ought to be a magic formula, and I searched for it. The river will never make it over the bank, I would tell myself, and then, into town the river would come. And then I'd tell myself that the river would be in town by daylight and I'd set and watch her creep inch by inch up the steep bank. Other times it would rise clear to the top of the bank would seem like it might burst over the top if even the smallest wave would push it. And then something would happen, and just like something had pushed a hole in her swollen side she would empty out and hurry down the bank."

Brad watched the old man closely now. The magic of the river was in his words.

"I walked and walked through these willows," the old man said, "trying to learn the secret. It seemed that about everything else that belonged to the river knew the answer but me. Now you take the kingfisher down the bank a piece. There has been one kingfisher or another in that hole inside the steep bank for as long as I can remember. And every kingfisher that ever lived there knew the answer I was searching for. Sometimes when I was the surest the river would fall I would watch the kingfisher glide from the hole and fly to higher ground. And then there were times that I thought the river would rise and I would watch the kingfisher set in the mouth of the hole when the water was within inches of coming into it. And the river would fall. The kingfisher sure enough knew the answer I was looking for. One day I caught the kingfisher studying the river. Now and then it would turn its head as if it were trying to hear something that the river was saying. I listened and listened, but all I could hear was the current in the water. I thought harder. Maybe it is in the current, I thought." The whine of a motor drifted through the willows and Dan Tackett turned his head for a minute and listened. Then he looked back at Brad and took a deep breath. "Maybe, too, I thought, it is the ears of the kingfisher. And what do you think, Brad?"

Brad studied the question, then he frowned. It seemed that Dan Tackett was always telling him of one of the secrets the river held. But he never completely told it. He always stopped and asked Brad to think about what he had said and try to give him an answer. This was a way for him to learn, according to the old man. He must learn to think about the river himself if he were ever to learn it. And most times it seemed to Brad that he would never learn it. He seldom gave the right answer.

Brad turned his head to one side and frowned harder. Again he did not know the answer. He knew the kingfisher only by sight. He did not really know the bird.

"I don't reckon I know," Brad said, tightening his lips.

"I was right," Dan Tackett said. "And as time passed I knew more than ever that I was right. The kingfisher was using both his eyes and his ears. With his eyes he was judging the surface of the water. If there was brush on it, he knew that it was a sure sign that the river was backing up and swelling. There had been a rain upriver to raise the water and wash the brush from the banks. With its eyes it was judging the amount of rain that had fallen and drained into the river. From the color of the water, it judged the current. Mud in water without a current will soon settle to the bottom and the water will become clear. Mud is heavier than water. But, if the water looks still and there is mud in it, it is a sign that the mud is coming out of smaller streams that are full and running out. This is a sign that there is water in the earth. The high hills along the shore of the Big Sandy have much to do with the river. If water soaks inside the earth, it must come out. And it comes out in the small creeks. So you see, Brad, the bird had learned much from the use of its keen eyes."

"But what about the ears of the kingfisher?" Brad asked.

"The ears!" Dan Tackett said, a smile bigger than ever coming to his face. "I learned that too. I reckon, Brad, the eyes of a bird or a human are not always keen enough. The surface of water might look calm and quiet. And yet, underneath all the time, a slow current might be pulling at the river. The eyes cannot see it. But the keen ears can hear it. When there is a current in the river the water is moving. There is but one way the current can move and that is down river, and so with a current the river is not apt to rise. It is when the main body of water is motionless that the rise is apt to come. There is nowhere for the water to go. And yet the creeks keep emptying in, adding more water to the river. It is only when the current comes again that the river will fall."

Dan Tackett leaned farther in his chair and brushed his hair from his face.

"Now you see, Brad," he said, "there is nothing magic about my knowledge of this river. I know more than the rest of the people in town because I have watched it closer. And I took time to think. Here along the river the world is slow. A man has time to think. There is no worry about progress or flood walls."

"But why does the town want the old flood wall?" Brad asked, quickly picking up the word.

"Don't reckon I have thought too much about that," Dan Tackett said, squinting his eyes. " I reckon I know one thing about it though. The flood wall will come along the top of the river bank. It will be built of dirt that comes from the river bank. With their trucks and bulldozers they will scrape the earth along the river until it is naked under the hot sun. The willows will be scraped from the ground. My home here is apt to be scraped along with them."

"Maybe we can stop the flood wall!" Brad said.

"Maybe," Dan Tackett said. "I just don't know."

Chapter 6

Brad left the old man's cabin after the sun began casting shadows of the brick buildings along the narrow streets in town. He hurried across the town, thinking how he might help Dan Tackett. Lost in his thoughts, he walked almost onto the porch of his home before he realized something was wrong. All of the lights were lit, including the light on the porch, which was seldom lit unless there was company.

Brad backed off the porch and walked into the yard where he could stand on his toes and see through the window. The room was full of people. It was a meeting, Brad thought, and this time they were meeting in his own house. They would be talking about the flood wall. He glanced back across the town toward the cabin of Dan Tackett. The shadows had gathered too low for him to see far.

Sitting in the chair on the porch of the cabin, Brad thought, would be Dan Tackett. He would be watching the same moon that Brad saw above the river—a moon redder than the hair of Captain Bozer. There would be a light wind in the willows, and the old man would be brushing the hair from his eyes. And perhaps he too would be thinking about the flood wall. Brad wondered what Dan Tackett would think if he knew Brad's mother was holding a flood-wall meeting in her house this very night.

Brad set his teeth, pulled his pants up tighter around his waist and walked in the front door.

At least a dozen people were in the room. They all looked at Brad as he walked in, and some of them spoke. After glancing quickly at their faces, he realized he did not know them all. A tall, dark-haired man sat at a small table in front of the group of people. On the table was stretched a large white paper with what looked like a map drawn on it. The dark-haired man looked up at Brad and smiled.

For some reason this man did not look strange to Brad. Brad felt sure that he had seen him somewhere before. He could not think where.

"Come here, Brad," his mother said, smiling across the room.

Brad edged closer into the room.

"I want you to meet Tom Hart," his mother said. "Mr. Hart is a government engineer, and he has come here to supervise the building of our flood wall for us."

"Well, now." The tall, dark-headed man rose and stretched out his hand. "I believe I have seen Brad before. He was staring at one of my trucks in town. I

waved at him." A smile came to Tom Hart's face. "And it seems to me that you didn't wave back. You were certainly doing a lot of staring."

Brad's face turned red. And now more than ever he wished that Dan Tackett were here to give him an answer. He had come face to face with the person that had come to destroy the world of Dan Tackett, and now he didn't know what to say.

Brad stood, his head down, staring at the floor.

"Well," his mother said, "what do you say about that, Brad?"

It seemed now to Brad that everyone in the room stared and waited for his answer. They waited for him to apologize to Tom Hart.

"I . . . I didn't see him," Brad said, glancing at Mr. Hart and then turning his head away.

"What on earth is the matter with you, Brad?" his mother asked. "Maybe it would be best if you were to go to your room."

Brad slowly turned to leave the room.

"Wait a minute," Tom Hart said.

Brad stopped and stared at the tall, dark-headed Mr. Hart. The man was smiling at him.

"Brad is right," he said. "He couldn't have really seen me. The sun was awful bright that day." He looked at Brad and winked. "It would have been impossible for

Brad to have seen me."

Brad's mother still stared at him. And in her eyes, Brad thought he saw a doubt as to what Tom Hart had just said.

"Well," she said, "it's getting late just the same. We have a lot to talk about here tonight. Perhaps it would still be best if you were to go to your room, Brad."

Brad turned to leave the room.

"Brad," Tom Hart said, "now that we have met, I hope we can become good friends. Perhaps you can come to the river up where we have begun the flood wall. There will be a lot to see, and I would enjoy having you."

Brad kept on walking, but he could hear still what was said.

"I hope you will excuse Brad," his mother said. "For some reason I believe he has the notion that the town is out to destroy Dan Tackett. Brad loves him even more than the rest of us. You might say Dan Tackett has taken the place of Brad's father."

"Then Dan Tackett is a lucky man," Brad heard Tom Hart say.

Once in his room Brad changed his clothes as quickly as he could. But he did not go to bed. Instead he stood as close to the wall of the room as he could get, and with his ear against it, he listened for every word.

Many times as they talked Brad wanted to slip his clothes on and sneak out of the house and hurry to the cabin of the old man. Dan Tackett, to Brad's way of thinking, was in serious trouble. The flood wall was a much larger foolish notion than either of them had thought, and it was to be built much faster. He listened while Tom Hart told the amount of dirt the bulldozers could raise in one scoop. And as he talked he told of the plans for up and down the river bank. Brad could not see, but he imagined Tom Hart was showing the people what he meant using the map that he had stretched on the table. Tears welled in Brad's eyes when Tom Hart spoke of the small section of land where the cabin of the old man stood. According to the plans, this land would have to be scraped clean, and a dirt wall would replace the willow trees.

When Brad heard a mention of Dan Tackett's name, he pressed so close to the wall that it hurt his ear.

"What shall we do about Dan Tackett?" someone asked.

The room was silent. Brad held his breath, and his heart beat faster than ever when he recognized the next voice as that of his mother.

"We have talked of this before," she said, slowly. "And we have gotten nowhere. I do not believe we can ever convince him that we need the flood wall. He is an old man. He must find the answer for himself. And . . . and I hope he finds the right one. I do not believe we can go on hiding from him what is happening, and he has got to go. Maybe he will understand. I hope so."

"I suppose I feel the same way the rest of the town does about Dan Tackett," another voice spoke up. "Once, if it hadn't been for the old man, the water of that river would have washed away all that I had. He fought the current in his joeboat and rowed all of my belongings to high land. I'll be grateful to him always, but now we must think of the flood wall and what it will mean to the town. I say that we cannot afford to wait for Dan Tackett to agree with us. I, for one, am tired of fighting the river. I believe we have discussed this before. Dan Tackett will have to move."

Brad backed away from the wall. He picked up his pants and pushed one leg through them, but then he stopped. He could sneak to the river, he thought. If his mother came into the room while he was gone she would know what had happened. She would assume that Brad had gone to the river to warn the old man. He knew that he must keep listening at the wall. In the morning he would travel to the river. And Dan Tackett would know the answer that would stop the town from moving him.

Then, after what seemed like hours, Brad heard the

people making ready to go. Tomorrow morning they would meet back in the town hall. Brad listened as they left. The last voice that he heard was that of Mr. Hart.

"I hope Brad will not dislike me," he said. "I hope he will understand what I have to do regarding the old man, Dan Tackett. I hope he won't think I do not respect the old man as the rest of the town does. But I cannot build a flood wall and save the cabin. If I should lose the friendship of the boy, I would have no excuse to visit with you again."

Brad heard his mother laugh.

"He will not dislike you," his mother answered. "One thing I have taught Brad is to think. He will need some time, just like Dan Tackett. But you are welcome to come visit us any time. You will not need Brad as an excuse."

Brad hurried as quickly as he could to get in bed. He pulled up the covers and closed his eyes.

"Brad," his mother's voice came to his ears as he felt her sit on the side of the bed.

Tears welled in Brad's eyes, and he tried to keep from sniffing. His throat was so dry that he could hardly swallow.

"I suppose that it is time that we talked," his mother said. "First, I am ashamed of the way you acted in front of Mr. Hart tonight."

"And . . . and he," Brad said, wiping his eyes, "ought to be ashamed wanting to scrape the cabin of Dan Tackett with his old bulldozer too." Then Brad caught his breath. His mother would know that he had listened. He raised up in the bed and stared at her with his eyes wide.

"It's all right, Brad," she said. "I knew you were listening all the time we talked. My ears are keen too."

Brad frowned. What did his mother mean about her ears being so keen? He wondered if she too knew of the keen ears that belonged to the kingfisher.

"But you see, Brad," she said, "he is not going to scrape up the home of Dan Tackett. He does not want to hurt the old man. All he wants is to put a flood wall around the town to protect us all from the river. He only needs the ground the cabin is sitting on." She paused. "I have asked you once to think about the flood wall and what it would mean. You have thought only of one side—the side of Dan Tackett. Did you ever stop to think that maybe for once Dan Tackett is wrong? I know that he has been right in many ways. But he is human too. I believe Dan Tackett will find his mistake. If you will only stop to think, it might be that you could help him find the answer he needs."

"Dan Tackett will find his answer," Brad said. "He was here long before the flood wall. And he has learned a few tricks too. He told me so."

"You are right," his mother said. "Dan Tackett was here before the flood wall, but Dan Tackett was also here before the first car came to town. He was against that too. He walked through the streets of the town warning against it, saying that it would blow up. It didn't. The car has helped us travel to many places we could not have otherwise seen. The cars are here to stay, and Dan Tackett has learned to live with them. One day he will look on the flood wall and accept it just as he did the car."

"But the car didn't take his home away from him," Brad said. "The river belongs to Dan Tackett. It is his home."

"But the river does not belong to Dan Tackett alone," his mother said. "The river belongs to us all. The good Lord made it free to all. It is just that Dan Tackett lives closer to it and understands it better."

"I'll bet He meant for it to belong to Dan Tackett," Brad said.

"I doubt that the Lord was even thinking of Dan Tackett when He made the river," his mother answered.

"And I'll bet He wasn't thinking of the flood wall either," Brad said. "Dan Tackett said if He had been, He would have put a flood wall around the town in the first place."

"But the Lord intended for us to do some of the work ourselves," his mother said. "He gave us the dirt and the machines and the knowledge."

"But Dan Tackett has got to stay on the river, Ma," Brad said, rubbing his eyes again. "Dan Tackett told me so. 'Look here, Dan Tackett,' he told me the Lord says to him one day as he was walking among the willows, 'you have got to learn this river. It must be your home for all the days you are here on earth. All of the good people of Catlettsburg will be depending on you to watch this river for them. You must not let the river rise and catch them asleep. This is your job.'" Tears came down Brad's cheeks. "And Dan Tackett has been working at it ever since," he said.

"And Dan Tackett has done a wonderful job, too," his mother said, "but one day Dan Tackett will be too old. Then what?"

"Dan Tackett says that by then I will know the river," Brad said. "And then I can have his job."

"But if we had the flood wall, Brad," his mother said, "you would not have to watch the river. And then you would be free to do another job for the town and its people."

"But I want to watch the river," Brad said, "just like Dan Tackett."

"I can see, Brad," his mother said, "that you have

done very little thinking about this flood wall. Without even thinking, you have tried to judge it. You have only thought what is good for two people: you and Dan Tackett. These are the thoughts of a selfish person. You must think of what is good for all." His mother shook her head. "I can only say to you that we mean no harm to Dan Tackett. I want you to know that the town loves him very much. And if he is the man I think he is, he will agree with us in the end."

Brad sat up farther in the bed.

"But if Dan Tackett has to move . . ." he began.

"Dan Tackett will have to move," his mother said. "But it is not as bad as you think. The town is going to move him, cabin and all. It will cost him nothing. We will move his cabin to a piece of property farther back against the hills. He will even be closer to you."

"But what if Dan Tackett don't want to move?" Brad asked.

Brad saw the frown come to his mother's face. She stared toward the window. He could see the streaks of gray hair from the light that came from the moon. There were even a few wrinkles on her face. Tonight he noticed them more than ever before.

"We can only hope that he does," his mother said.

His mother left the room.

Brad lay awake. Every time he closed his eyes

thoughts came to him. Once he seemed to see Tom Hart grinning from the seat of a giant bulldozer. The large blade on the bulldozer scooped up the cabin of Dan Tackett and whirled it into the air. Next he saw the great flood wall, so high that the top of it disappeared into the clouds. On the other side of the wall, he thought he could hear the voice of Dan Tackett. He was calling for Brad. But the wall was too steep for Brad to climb. The world of Dan Tackett was closed off from him forever.

Brad shook his head. And when he closed his eyes again, he saw the green leaves of the willows along the river. They blew in a warm wind. The river had stretched out to sleep, and under a bright moon, the small catbird, Cindy, sat in the nest in the forks of the giant willow, her head sticking out over the nest. The old man sat in his chair on the porch, his arms folded and a smile on his face. The deep wrinkles in his face looked like the bark of the old willow more than ever tonight. And while the town slept, the old man quietly watched the river as he had done for many years. He listened and looked with ears and eyes as keen as those of the kingfisher. He was doing the job the Lord had given him.

Brad knew that he must fall asleep. He would have to be up early and hurry to the river. He must warn Dan Tackett. Thinking of the river was the fastest way to find sleep. It always was.

Chapter 7

Morning came. Before the sun had squinted the first time above the rim of the hills behind his house, Brad was up.

What would Dan Tackett think of the news Brad would bring? Would he know the answer? Once again Brad thought of the flood wall. What could Dan Tackett do? he wondered. How could he stop the giant blades of the bulldozer? Dan Tackett would not move from the river, of this Brad was sure. The river was his home, and the old man would not have it taken away from him. He had been there long before the bulldozers, and he would be there long after the bulldozers and trucks had gone.

Then, for the first time, Brad felt a small shiver of doubt. He remembered what his mother had told him of the automobiles. At first Dan Tackett had been greatly against them, but he had changed. In fact, Brad recalled that Dan Tackett had told him once what a wonderful thing the automobile was, hauling so many people about.

Brad frowned. There was a great deal of difference between a car and a flood wall. The car had nothing to do at all with the river. And the old man had at least had a choice. But it would not be so easy with the flood wall. The flood wall, whether he liked it or not, would be coming to take his home away.

Brad ate his breakfast slowly, and he hardly spoke to his mother. When he had finished eating, he was anxious to get out of the house.

At the door his mother called to him.

"Brad," she said. "I do not ask you to keep secret what you overheard last night; it would be a real burden. However, there is a promise I would like for you to make. It will not be asking too much."

Brad stood at the door with his head down. He could only hope that his mother did not ask him to make a choice between her opinion and that of Dan Tackett.

"I have asked you, Brad," his mother said, walking toward the door, "more than once to think about the flood wall and what it will mean to Catlettsburg. I know that you haven't. I ask now that you promise to think about it. Take all the time you need. And when you feel that you have found your answer, tell me exactly what you think of the flood wall. The answer must come through your own eyes and not the eyes of Dan Tackett."

For a moment Brad felt a great relief. He stared at

the door, weighing the promise that his mother had asked him to give to her. He did not think the promise would be hard. He could think of the flood wall. In fact, he had thought much about it since the first word had come to Catlettsburg.

Anxious to get out of the house and over to the river, he looked quickly at his mother.

"All right," he said. "I promise."

"Then that is all I ask," his mother said, smiling.

Chapter 8

As Brad walked through the yard, he glanced over his shoulder at the top of the hills behind him. The sun was high; already it had come over the steep ridge. The old man, Brad knew, would be sitting in his chair out in the yard, warmed by the streaks of sunlight that sifted through the leaves of the willows.

Dan Tackett could look at the sun any time, gauge its height, and tell how far into the day he was. It was the position of the sun that told the time. Now as Brad looked up, squinting his eyes, he could see that the sun was high. He would be late getting to the river. He had hoped to get there by daylight this morning. He hurried across town.

Already the streets in town had begun to show signs that the flood wall had come for sure. Heavy trucks hauling dirt back and forth had carried much of the soft river earth on their tires and had left thin layers of it along the streets. During the heat of the day, the sun had dried the moist earth into powder, and the wind had picked it up and cast it against the buildings that stood along both sides of the streets.

For the first time Brad noticed the stillness that was

there. The buildings looked older than ever before. Down the street he saw two men loading a large truck. They were emptying another of the buildings along the river. It was then that Brad thought he knew why the stillness was around him. He looked in a low window of the building closest to him and saw that it already was empty. The flood wall, he knew, would reach this far up the bank. He realized that the oldest buildings in town would be torn away by the bulldozers.

He thought of the flood wall again and of the promise he had made to his mother. He frowned. He understood now that his mother had asked a hard thing. The eyes of Dan Tackett would be of no use to him at all if he were to judge the flood wall for himself. And for a moment he felt himself trying to think how the flood wall could really help the town. He tried to see the many changes his mother had spoken about. In one way they all seemed to be good changes, and the town would be happy with them. That is, all but Dan Tackett. Suddenly he felt ashamed of his thoughts. What if Dan Tackett knew what he was thinking?

Brad tightened his mouth and stared toward the river. He became more determined than before that he would not be fooled by the modern ways that would destroy the world he loved. He would stand with Dan Tackett.

But as he walked past the buildings, he had a feeling of guilt. Once before he had made another promise. He had promised old Dan Tackett that he would always be judged by his word. He must never lie or break a promise to anyone. A promise must be kept always because it was a true way to judge a man's character. Yet if he kept the promise to his mother, he would have to try to prove that the world of Dan Tackett was wrong, or at least that Dan Tackett was wrong this time. This was all too much to think about.

He turned over the top of the river bank toward the cabin.

Chapter 9

Brad had no more started over the bank when he stopped. There was something wrong. He stared through the willows toward the cabin.

A long path had been cleared near the top of the river bank, making a path as straight as an ash tree both up and down the river as far as Brad could see. Many of the small willow saplings that grew near the top of the river bank had been cut. Brad took a deep breath. The path had been cut in a direct line with the cabin of the old man.

Brad hurried along the bank. He stopped again. The stub of a willow sapling that had been cut poked its white flesh toward the sun, not tall enough now to stick above the blades of grass that sprinkled the riverbank. Brad knelt beside it and rubbed his fingers over the jagged top. There was sap still oozing out, enough to wet the end of his fingers. This tree had been freshly cut.

Brad rose to his feet and started to leave. Then he stopped again. In the center of the path, a square wooden peg made of white pine had been driven into the earth.

Brad ran down the bank to the cabin.

"Dan Tackett!" Brad hollered as he stepped into the small yard. A swirl came from the giant willow above his head, and he looked to see the small catbird, Cindy, glide out of the tree toward the river. His voice had frightened her.

"Howdy, Brad," Dan Tackett said from his chair on the porch. "Wondered if they'd let you come today."

Brad walked to the porch.

"Ma knows I am here," he said. "Ma don't care for me coming."

"Guess not," Dan Tackett said. "I figured all of this excitement over the flood wall might make a difference. Don't know as I would rightly blame her myself."

Brad eyed the old man, not quite sure that he understood the meaning of his words. It was true, he thought, his mother had her mind set on the flood wall, but she would never stop him from coming to the cabin.

Dan Tackett stepped off the porch and walked to where a white-pine peg had been driven in the ground in his yard.

"Look," he said, hoarsely.

He eyed the peg for a minute and then kicked it hard with his brogan shoe. The peg split and a few splinters from it flew into the air.

Seeing the old man angry, Brad ran to the peg. He knelt beside it and pulled as hard as he could. The peg did not move at all. It was solid in the ground.

"No use, Brad," Dan Tackett said, quieter now. "They will just drive another one even if you can pull this one up. I have tried it already this morning."

"But . . . but what is it for?" Brad asked.

The old man leaned against the giant willow and looked upriver.

"They came early this morning," the old man said. "There was two of them. And they cleared the path as they came. They would clear a piece, and then they would stop and drive a peg. Above them, farther upriver, stood a man looking through a telescope that stood on a three-legged stand. This man would wave his hand down river as the two men drove the pegs into the ground. They would watch him and move the peg like he showed them. Right in line with the cabin they came, then here in the yard they stopped to drive a peg." Dan Tackett pointed. "And right behind them I came. I pulled the peg from my yard."

"And what did they say?" Brad asked, his eyes growing wide.

"Nothing much," Dan Tackett said, a frown coming to his face. "They didn't even argue. They just looked at me and smiled. 'Morning, Dan Tackett,' they said to me. And this time they drove the peg so far into the ground I could not pull it out."

"Well," Brad said, squinting his eyes, "I guess you showed them anyway, Dan Tackett."

"Nope," Dan Tackett said. "Can't say as how I did at all. I wanted to though, Brad, powerful hard. But I knew if I had pulled the second peg they would have drove the third one deeper. I reckon we are just in for a heap of trouble."

"Shucks, Dan Tackett," Brad said, frowning. "A little old wooden peg is nothing, I reckon."

"Maybe," Dan Tackett said. "A lot depends, I reckon, on what the peg is being driven there for. This one is to mark the path of the flood wall. This is where they are figuring on putting it up."

Tears welled in Brad's eyes. He looked up the cleared path as far as he could see. Sure enough, he knew, the path had been cleared in a direct line with the cabin. If the wall followed the path, the dirt would cover up the home of Dan Tackett. Unless . . . and suddenly Brad thought of what his mother had said about the town moving the cabin back against the hill.

"I got something to tell you, Dan Tackett," Brad quickly said. "I used my ears just like you asked for me to do. And I sure heard a lot, a powerful lot."

Dan Tackett bent his ear away from the wind and listened closely as Brad talked on. Here and there he shook his head. When Brad got to the part about the plan to move Dan Tackett, he stopped. He did not really know why, but he could not tell this.

"It is bad news, Brad," Dan Tackett said. "But by-doggies it took a mighty keen ear to catch that much so soon. With ears that keen, I wouldn't be surprised if the kingfisher itself didn't start depending on you."

Brad smiled at this.

"I reckon," Dan Tackett said, "being as how me and you are partners, I ought to tell you what I learned this morning myself." He looked again out over the river. "After the two men walked on this morning another man came. He was a tall, dark-headed man. Said his name was Tom Hart and that he was an engineer and that he was going to build the flood wall."

Brad's face turned red and he turned away so that Dan Tackett could not see him blush. Brad had not mentioned Tom Hart.

"He looked to be as straight as an ash tree and had the blackest hair I ever saw," Dan Tackett continued. "And what do you suppose, Brad, this man says to me?"

Brad thought of Tom Hart, the engineer, and of the map that had outlined the destruction of Dan Tackett's world.

"He told me," Dan Tackett said, "that I would have to move. Said he was mighty sorry, and so was the rest of the town. He said he figured that I would understand." Dan Tackett scowled. "They sent a stranger to tell me that I would have to leave the river, and then expected me to understand. They had a piece of ground for me back across town near the foot of the hill. And he says: 'When could you be ready to move?' And I looks at him and says: 'How long would it take you with your bulldozers and trucks to move that river out there?'" Dan Tackett looked over the river and made a wide sweep of his hand. "This Tom Hart looked toward the river. 'What has moving the river got to do with it?' he says. 'The river is my home,' I said. 'And I intend to be right here where this cabin is setting the day the good Lord calls me to come away from it.'"

"And you will, too!" Brad said. "That's what I told Ma. And . . . and she didn't think you would, Dan Tackett." Brad caught his breath. He had not intended to tell Dan Tackett of the way his mother felt about the flood wall. He looked quickly at Dan Tackett. "But . . . but Ma is a woman. And women don't know much about the river, do they, Dan Tackett?"

"That's right," Dan Tackett said. "Course your ma is not just an ordinary woman. She is a fine woman, and you ought to be mighty proud of her. I reckon she would do what she felt was right."

"But why, then," Brad asked, "would she think it was right for you to move just so they can build an old flood wall?"

"It is not just your mother," Dan Tackett said. "The rest of the town is thinking the same way. But what can the town know of the feelings an old man might carry in his heart? Ain't no one, I reckon, excepting maybe you, Brad, that knows how I feel about this here river. You know how I stand as far as the flood wall is concerned. I have never been for modern things. People used to walk and now they ride. They ain't got time enough to know the beauty of the river and the hills like they used to. They are moving faster than this river moves during a washout. They ain't got the time to stop along the way to catch a good breath of air. They don't have time to think. They try to make a machine that will do their thinking for them." Dan Tackett brushed his hair out of his eyes.

"But what can we do?" Brad asked.

"I am going to stand my ground!" Dan Tackett said. "I am too old to pull up and move. If they intend to take this piece of land, they will have to scrape me off."

"And they will scrape me too!" Brad said, wiping his eyes.

Dan Tackett grinned and patted Brad on the shoulder.

"I believe you'd stay at that," he said. "But I want you to listen close to me, Brad."

Brad looked into the face of the old man. He had the feeling that something was wrong.

"You are a true friend, Brad," Dan Tackett said. "The only one here in town I have left, I reckon. But I reckon this is really a fight for an old man that has got nothing at all to lose. And . . . I reckon, too, it just might be a fight that I am going to lose. Now, I couldn't ask that you stand and fight on a losing side, could I?"

Brad wiped his eyes quickly. He wanted more than anything to speak but a lump came inside his throat. He wanted Dan Tackett to know more than ever that he was surely on his side. He did not think of the town now. He hated the word "progress" more than all the other words he knew.

"How do you know we will lose?" Brad said at last.

"This Mr. Hart made it very clear this morning," Dan Tackett said. "He carried the word of the town with him. He talked to me just like I was now so old and useless that I couldn't help myself. The town wanted to move me! Like I couldn't move myself if I took a notion. I'll show them. I ain't so old I have to be looked after."

"How do you know he can make you leave, Dan Tackett?" Brad asked, as he looked around the yard of the cabin. Brad was not set to give up.

"Well," Dan Tackett said, "Mr. Hart had a paper from Mayor Tumbles that was asking me to move. I reckon he could take me to court. Tom Hart says the law states if the town decides to build something that most everyone thinks is for the good of the town, the town has the right to build it. If there is something in the way of the building, say like this cabin of mine they have the right to offer me a settlement of some kind for it. In this case, they have offered to move me free of charge and give me a piece of free land to live on. If I refuse, then they take my cabin anyway. What I can't figure is how can the law buy the feelings that an old man carries in his heart?"

"But what if you still don't move?" Brad asked. "What will they do then?"

"I reckon that is what I intend to find out," Dan Tackett said.

Dan Tackett put his arm around Brad's shoulder. "You ain't ever going to be in the way," Dan Tackett said. "But I figured it wasn't right for me to ask you to fight a fight that might not be yours at all."

"But it is, Dan Tackett," Brad said. "I love this river, too. I would be powerful lonely without you and Captain Bozer.

Dan Tackett rubbed his hand through his hair.

"Well," he said, "I wouldn't be wanting to get your ma mad at me, Brad. Wouldn't want her to think that I was maybe putting ideas in your head. Your ma has been trusting you with me for a long time now, and you have been great company to me."

"But Ma says that I can make up my own mind." Brad said. "And I reckon I have it made up too. I want to stay with you, Dan Tackett."

"Well," Dan Tackett said, 'being as how this is the case I reckon I am a lucky man after all having as good a friend as you left in the town. Just one thing"—Dan squinted his eyes—"no matter what is to happen here along the river, you are to let me handle it alone. You must promise me this."

Brad looked toward the river and then back at the old man. It seemed to him that all he had been doing lately was making promises. It seemed also to him that Dan Tackett was trying to find a way to keep him out of trouble. Brad looked at Dan Tackett.

"I promise," he said.

Chapter 10

In the days that followed, it was quiet in the town, broken only by the hum of the motors of the giant trucks and bulldozers. Dust settled thick on the buildings along the streets.

Twice during the week, Tom Hart came to Brad's house to have supper with them. Or rather he came to have supper with Brad's mother. Brad wanted no part of him. But Brad strained his ears for any word Mr. Hart might say that concerned moving the cabin of the old man from the river. However, there was little talk of it, in fact nothing that Brad had not already heard. By now Brad began to feel that maybe the town had given up the foolish notion of moving Dan Tackett.

But Dan Tackett was not as sure as Brad. He moved along the banks of the river as restless as a catbird. Each day he began to sneak upriver to eye the progress of the flood wall. And between his trips, he kept his eyes peeled toward the sand bar for Captain Bozer.

When Captain Bozer came out of the river, the bar had not built up, and there was a wide channel in the river. Dan Tackett had not had to light the lantern even though Captain Bozer had passed during the early morning before daylight. On his return trip up the river, he stopped again to talk with Dan Tackett. Again he told Dan Tackett not to worry about the flood wall. He looked at Brad and laughed.

"Keep your eyes peeled to the sand bar, Brad," he had said. "Dan Tackett may be off chasing a flood wall. And these old bones of mine tell me that rain and fog are not far away. You might have to light the lantern."

The day came too on which Cindy's eggs popped open and three small birds, their bills stretched toward the warm sun, peeped hungrily in the giant willow. And Brad sat during the day watching Cindy dig in the soft earth along the river for worms that she carried back to the nest. Now and then she swooped low to the earth and grabbed a yellow grasshopper that had stopped too long to play his fiddle and chew his tobacco on the stalk of a horseweed.

Brad wondered if Cindy would return next spring to the giant willow. And then a frown came to his face. Would there be a willow here for the bird to return to? He turned his eyes toward the large mound of earth that could be seen now from the porch of the cabin. The flood wall had moved fast. Before long, it would be next to the cabin, and then the real fight would come. Or would the fight really come ahead of the flood wall like the path that held the white-pine pegs? There was no way to know just how long it would be.

But the answer came quickly. And it came more quietly than the water of the Big Sandy River could creep up the bank and sneak into town.

Brad had dressed early and had hurried to beat the shadows of the sun across town. Today he and Dan Tackett had planned to take the joeboat and paddle out to the sand bar where they would spend the day fishing for white perch.

Beside the last row of brick buildings that faced the river, he stopped. Several men were standing on top of the bank looking down where the cabin stood. A large truck with a long bed and a hoist on it had backed to the edge of the bank. From the hoist hung a large cable. Beside this truck sat another truck with a larger flat bed.

Tom Hart came to the top of the bank, walked over to the truck with the hoist, and said something to the man seated in it. Then he walked to the side of the truck, said something and signaled with his hand. The truck backed as close to the edge of the river bank as it could. The cable was lowered in the back. Two more men hurried over the bank and the long-bed truck pulled closer.

Brad could hear Mr. Hart giving orders.

Brad sneaked to the end of the building without being seen. From there he could stand on his toes and see the cabin. Tears welled in his eyes.

The small cabin had been moved from the earth and rested on two large wooden ties under either end of it. Cables had been fastened to the end of the ties, pulled up over the cabin roof and joined. A man climbed to the roof of the cabin and hooked the cables together and then hooked them onto the end of the hoist cable.

Brad could not believe his eyes. Dan Tackett still sat in his chair on the small front porch. The old man's lips were pressed tightly together, his eyes set upon the river, his arms folded defiantly across his chest.

"Easy now," Tom Hart said, and the hoist growled as the small cabin rose slowly from the earth.

Dan Tackett still sat motionless, his arms folded. The cabin hovered in the air close to the trunk of the giant willow. Brad saw Cindy stick her head over the side of the nest. She looked at Dan Tackett so close now, sitting on the porch, and she sent her catcall voice through the willows. Into the air she zoomed nearly hitting Dan Tackett. She circled the nest, whirling back and forth, just missing the old man each time she passed. By this time, the cabin had soared almost as high as the tree.

"Evicting you too, Cindy!" the old man said, ducking the catbird. Then he folded his arms tighter and set his jaw.

The cabin swung over the top of the river bank, and the hoist slowly lowered it to the bed of the truck that was waiting. A few people had gathered along the top of the bank, and they stared at the old man. But Dan Tackett did not move even when the cable from the hoist was released from the top of the cabin and the two trucks started slowly across town.

Brad walked along the edge of the buildings as fast as he could, trying to keep up with the trucks. Tears welled in his eyes until he could hardly see. He squinted, trying to push out the tears, but more tears came in their place. He tried to keep hidden. He did not want Dan Tackett to see him. Brad felt he had let the old man down. Surely if they had planned to move the cabin today, he should have known. He was sure that his mother knew of it, and she had said nothing about it. Still, it had been his job to know. The plans to move the cabin had been made in town, and he had missed them.

Across the town, they hauled Dan Tackett and his cabin. Brad watched as people came out to stare.

At the piece of ground against the hill, they swung the cabin down, and Dan Tackett still said nothing. Brad stood beside the giant oak that shaded the cabin and watched the trucks back and pull away. At last, he turned away and walked toward his home.

The distance to the house seemed to Brad to be the longest he had ever walked. All around him seemed to be an empty world. What would happen now to Dan Tackett? He did not know the answer, and the more he thought about it the more tears came to his eyes. He remembered over and over again the things the old man had said to him. Dan Tackett had to have something to do. His job was watching the river. When the time came that the town no longer needed him, there would be no reason for him to stay on the earth. Brad could not stand to think of the old man's leaving. He wondered if this was how the world of progress came. He remembered how the old man said in the world of progress there was no time to stop and catch a breath of air. Brad was more than ever determined to have no part of progress. If Dan Tackett was ever to leave, then he knew that he wanted to leave with him. He would tell his mother so.

Once at his house, Brad walked straight to his room. He stood beside the window staring toward the river. He could see the tops of the willows weaving in the river wind. But the river seemed to have little meaning now. There was no river at all without Dan Tackett.

He heard his mother come into the room. He did not turn to face her.

"You are home early," his mother said.

"They have hauled Dan Tackett away," Brad said, his voice trembling. "And you knew they would."

"I knew," his mother said, walking closer to him. "It was the only thing left to do. You must try to understand. Have you been with Dan Tackett?"

"I am ashamed to see Dan Tackett," Brad said. "They moved his cabin away, and I couldn't help him at all."

Brad pressed his face to the window and stared.

"The world has not come to an end, Brad," his mother said. "The world has not ended for Dan Tackett. There is a new world for him. And the old man will find his place in it, too, if I am any judge."

"But there is no place for him to go now," Brad said, facing his mother for the first time.

"Well," his mother said, "maybe you are right. But you see, Brad, I thought you were a true friend of Dan Tackett's."

Brad frowned and looked hard at his mother.

"I am," he said. "And I will always be, too."

"Are you, Brad?" his mother asked. "If you were a true friend, would you turn your back on him now? This is the time he needs your company the most."

"But what can I do?" Brad asked.

"You can go to him," his mother answered. "He will be a lonely man until he finds his new place. You can help him to find it. You must agree with him that the old ways have been good ways but that they have been stepping stones for better ones. Maybe he can see that the flood wall is for the good of all. We can have the river around us and close it off when it becomes angry. Right now Dan Tackett needs your company more than anything else in the world."

Thinking that Dan Tackett might be needing him made Brad feel better. He wiped his eyes with his shirt sleeve. And then he looked at his mother.

"But why," he asked slowly, "would you be for Dan Tackett now?"

His mother grinned and brushed her hair from her face. "I have never been against him, Brad," she said. "This shows that you have not bothered to think about it, and perhaps to think about a lot of other things. But now you must think. You must surely think about the flood wall. Your promise must be kept. Somewhere in your thinking about the flood wall will lie the answer for Dan Tackett.

"One more thing, Brad," his mother said. "Do not let on to Dan Tackett that you feel sorry for him because of what has happened. You must show Dan Tackett that you have all the faith in the world that there is room for him and the flood wall too. It just might be that the faith you have will give him the encouragement he needs to search for his place in the new world."

Chapter 11

It seemed strange now to Brad that his trip to the cabin of Dan Tackett should not take him across the small town of Catlettsburg to the river.

As Brad walked to the cabin he thought of how he might approach the old man. "Howdy, Dan Tackett," he thought he might say. He knew that he must seem happy when he walked up to Dan Tackett, or it would only add to the sadness of the old man. Perhaps, he thought, he could just act like nothing at all had ever happened—just like the cabin had always sat there against the foot of the hills. But this would be hard for him to do. The hills were just not the river. And that was that. The black oaks and locusts along the slopes did not look like the willows. And through them the wind sang a different song.

Brad thought and thought until he found himself almost face to face with the old man at the cabin. He stopped and looked toward him. Dan Tackett still sat on the porch, but his arms were no longer crossed. Instead his hands lay in his lap, and from where Brad stood he could see the old man rubbing them hard against one another.

Brad looked quickly around him as he walked into the yard. It was true that this place was not the river, but it was not an ugly place. A small hollow sliced through the hills and came down close to the left side of the cabin. And through the hollow ran a small creek. From where Brad stood he could hear the water humming over the sandrock bed. And near the cabin black oak trees grew close enough to offer their shade.

"Shucks, Dan Tackett," Brad said, "I reckon we still ain't too far away from the river. I can hear it in the creek over there."

Dan Tackett looked up. A smile came to his face. He squinted his eyes and then the smile disappeared.

"No satisfaction to it," he said. "No satisfaction at all."

The old man glanced toward the small creek. They sat in silence for a time.

"I didn't hear them, Dan Tackett!" Brad burst out. "I was trying hard, but I didn't hear them say they were going to move you! I reckon it is all my fault!"

"Now, Brad," the old man said, moving from his chair and walking over to where Brad sat on the edge. "Weren't no fault of yours. It was just bound to happen. Reckon I would have liked to have spent my last days along the banks of the river, though."

"But . . . but there ought to be lots of things a man

as smart as you can do, Dan Tackett."

"Nope," Dan Tackett said. "Ain't much use of a man fighting the signs. And the signs say that about all my time is used up. All I can do now, I reckon, is to set here and wait."

"But what will you wait for, Dan Tackett?"

"For the good Lord to call me," Dan Tackett said. "What else is there to be waiting for? He give me a job once, and the job is finished."

Brad wiped his eyes. The old man squinted at him.

"Ain't there nothing we can do?" Brad asked. "Nothing at all?"

Dan Tackett rubbed his chin and scratched his head. Brad watched the old man closely now, hoping that he would answer.

"Well," he said, "I reckon there is one thing left we could do. I would like to take just one last look at the river over there before the good Lord takes me away. Just something to remember while I'm setting here a waiting. Reckon you could go with old Dan Tackett if you had a mind to."

Brad could not answer. But he wished that the old man would not talk this way.

"Tell you what, Brad," Dan Tackett said, squinting at the hills above him," you come first thing in the morning. Don't know how long it will be before they scrape the river bank where my home used to be. And I want to see it just like I have always knowed it."

Brad sat on the porch of the cabin until the shadows crept down the hills and covered the yard. And promising the old man again that he would be there early in the morning, he turned to go.

"One more thing, Brad," Dan Tackett said. "You can tell your ma and the rest of the town something. Tell them that their old friend Dan Tackett has set down here at his cabin waiting. Waiting for the good Lord to take him from the earth. You watch their eyes now, Brad. Let old Dan Tackett know how they act."

Brad walked along the foot of the hills toward home.

His mother met him at the door.

"Well," she asked, "how did things go?"

"Dan Tackett has given up," Brad said, and he walked quickly to his room.

His mother followed.

"All that is needed then is for you to give up, isn't it, Brad?" she said. "And then the fight will be over for Dan Tackett."

Chapter 12

As Brad dressed, he watched the rim of the hills. The sun had not yet winked above them. The morning was early, and he should make it to the cabin of Dan Tackett before the sun was high. His mother was up early, too, and he could hear her in the kitchen fixing breakfast.

She talked very little while Brad ate, except now and then she smiled at him across the table. It was not until Brad started to leave that she spoke.

"You know, Brad," she said, cleaning off the table, "I am happy that my son is not a quitter."

On his way to the cabin Brad thought guiltily of the promise he had made to his mother. And he knew that he had not yet thought of the flood wall. At least not in the way she had asked. He remembered more than ever now that she had told him that he would have to think of it if he was to find the answer for the old man.

Dan Tackett stood at the cabin waiting. He squinted his eyes up at the sun that was trying to come over the rim of the hills behind the cabin.

"Reckon we had better be on our way," he said to Brad.

It was a slow trip across town. Dan Tackett was old

and today he limped worse than Brad had ever noticed before. When he came to the row of brick buildings that had faced the river for so long, he leaned his arm against the side of one and brushed the hair from his face.

"Remember when they built these buildings," he said. "Never knowed back then that we would both be leaving at the same time."

Under the shade of the willows the old man sat down where his cabin had once stood. He took a deep breath. And the first time he smiled was when he saw the gray catbird, Cindy, fly into the limbs of the giant willow. He knew that her young were safe, at least for a little while. She too, he said, had been forced from her slow life among the willows to a fast life now that the flood wall was here. She would have to speed up the growth of her young or be pushed out of the nest.

The hum of the trucks was loud on the river bank. But for some reason it did not bother Brad as much as it had once. He had gotten used to them, he figured. And he thought that maybe Dan Tackett had too. He seemed to pay them no mind.

Most of the time the old man watched the sky. Gray clouds hovered over the water. There was a wind in the limbs of the trees. He stopped once to watch the small catbird flap her wings as she lit on a limb of the giant

willow, and tried to hold her balance against the brisk wind that had come so quickly to the river.

"Clouds are gathering," Dan Tackett said to Brad, squinting his eyes beyond the tops of the willows.

"What does it mean?" Brad asked.

"Only one thing it could mean if they keep gathering," the old man said. "Rain!"

Dan Tackett had no more than spoken than the call of the rain crow drifted through the trees from somewhere down river.

"Hear that!" the old man said, cocking his ear. "There is the sure sign."

"Will the river come over the banks, Dan Tackett?" Brad asked, looking quickly upriver toward the steep dirt wall that he could see. "Would it come maybe high enough to wash the flood wall away?"

Dan Tackett squinted his eyes toward the wall.

"Nope," he said. "The river will not come over the banks in May. I have seen it reach near the top. I have seen it swift, muddy, and full of brush. But seldom have I seen it creep over the top of the banks." The old man looked at the sky again. "The rain is still not too close yet. Now let's see. Captain Bozer has made his turn at the upper end of the river. He is coming down the Kentucky side." The old man rubbed his chin. "With luck he should make it through a wide, deep channel."

Later, it seemed to Brad as if the day had sped past. He stood on top of the river bank beside the old man watching the evening shadows dance along the surface of the river. Here and there among the willows, a bird, trying to find a bed for the night, flew through the trees. He glanced at the river, and he thought of Captain Bozer. What would Captain Bozer think when he came to the mouth of the river and saw that the cabin of Dan Tackett was gone? If Captain Bozer blew his whistle, there would be no one to hear it. If the channel should not be clear, there would be no one to warn him. There might not even be a willow for the warning lantern to hang on should the channel be narrow.

Dan Tackett had become as quiet as the river. He stood looking over it, a solemn look on his wrinkled face. Then he turned and took a deep breath.

"I am ready to go," he said.

The old man limped across the town. He did not stop once. He walked even faster than before. Brad tried to keep up; he felt tears come to his eyes, but he hid them from Dan Tackett.

Back at the cabin Dan Tackett took his seat in the chair and folded his arms again.

"What . . . what will we do now, Dan Tackett?" Brad asked.

"Nothing more to do now but wait," Dan Tackett

said. "I am ready any time the Lord is."

Brad turned and faced the old man. Tears streamed down his face, and he did not care if Dan Tackett saw them. He walked slowly toward the chair of the old man.

"But I don't want you to go, Dan Tackett," he said. And he buried his face in his hands.

Dan Tackett stretched from his chair and put his arm around Brad, and they walked together to the edge of the porch.

"By-doggies, Brad," Dan Tackett said, "I don't reckon you are making it easier for me to want to go. But can't you see? There ain't no reason why I should hang around here in people's way. Now you just try to pretend that old Dan Tackett is fixing to take a long trip somewhere, and me and you will face this thing together like we have always done things before."

Brad wiped his eyes and sniffed.

"All right, Dan Tackett," he said. "I'll try."

"That's the way, Brad," Dan Tackett said, sympathetically.

"I . . . I can still come tomorrow, can't I, Dan Tackett?" Brad asked. "You won't go before then, will you?"

"Hard to tell," Dan Tackett answered. "Don't know how long I will have to wait. Far as I am concerned I am ready now."

Brad walked away silently. There seemed to be nothing more to say. He desperately needed time to think.

Brad did not go into the house when he reached home. Instead he sat on the step of his porch and looked into the night. The wind was heavier in the trees, and the moon was gliding through great black clouds, sprinkling light now and then toward the earth like the flicker of a lightning bug.

He did not hear his mother until she was all the way to the end of the porch and sitting beside him.

"Is there something wrong, Brad?" she asked.

"Dan Tackett is leaving," Brad said. "He is leaving because of the flood wall."

"Leaving!" his mother said. "But where is he going?"

"He is going to leave the earth," Brad said. He sniffed and cleared his throat. "He is only waiting until the Lord makes a place for him. If he has to wait long, he is going to ask the Lord to hurry it up a little."

"I see," his mother said, and a smile came to her face.

Brad saw the smile and frowned.

"You shouldn't laugh at Dan Tackett," Brad said.

"But I am not laughing at Dan Tackett," she said. "Why should I laugh at the ways of an old person? There are streaks of gray in my hair already. But tell me, Brad. When did Dan Tackett say he was leaving for sure?"

"He is not too sure yet," Brad answered. "But it will not be long. He may not even be there tomorrow when I go to the cabin." Brad wiped his eyes again.

"Well," his mother said, "you still might have a little time left."

"Time for what?" Brad asked, turning to face his mother.

His mother rubbed her face and thought.

"I am not too sure just right now," she said. "But maybe time to find a job here for Dan Tackett."

"But where could I look, Ma?" Brad asked.

"I am not too sure right now," his mother said.

A frown came to Brad's face and he stared at his mother.

"You have not given up, have you, Brad?" she asked.

Brad looked away. He squinted his eyes toward the river. He could not see across the town. The moon was gone.

"No," he said.

"Good," his mother answered. "Then we still have a chance."

Chapter 13

He left the house at daylight and hurried toward the cabin. And as the cabin came into sight, he stopped to catch his breath. Dan Tackett was not on the porch. Brad swallowed hard.

"Dan Tackett!" Brad hollered, as he hurried into the yard.

No answer came.

"Dan Tackett!" Brad hollered again, louder. A choke came to his voice.

Brad could not holler the third time. His throat was filled with a lump and tears came to his eyes. He looked around the small cabin for any signs of tracks. He looked along the foot of the hills. And as he stared along the soft earth, he remembered that Dan Tackett had told him once that when the day came that he was too old to do any more for the people and the town, he intended to climb to the top of the tallest willow and step into a cloud. And as the cloud drifted over the Big Sandy River, he would poke out his head and take one last look. But now with his cabin against the side of the hills, he would not have a willow to climb. He could, Brad thought, walk up the steep slope. The tops of the hills looked mighty close to the clouds today.

If Dan Tackett had really been telling the truth about stepping into a cloud, Brad thought, today would be a bad day to leave. The clouds were blacker than a lump of coal. But if the old man had walked up the steep hillside, there should be tracks, because the earth was soft under the limbs of the oaks. There were no tracks to be seen.

A small trail of smoke came from the chimney of the cabin and drifted low along the yard and then rose and sailed off with the wind. Brad's heart beat fast.

"Dan Tackett!" he hollered again.

The old man stuck his head through the door.

"Had your breakfast yet?" Dan Tackett asked.

Brad walked into the cabin and watched the old man kindle the new fire in the stove in the corner of the room. He pulled off an old blue granite coffeepot and poured a cup of coffee in a cup that sat on the table. And as he ate and drank his coffee, he looked at Brad.

"Wind must be getting keener," he said. "Enough to cut tears in a man's eyes."

Brad wiped his eyes quickly.

"Reckon," he said. "I am glad to see you, Dan Tackett. I am mighty glad that you are still here."

"Well," Dan Tackett said, taking another sip of the coffee, "reckon this getting things ready could take a little more time than I had planned on."

"Ma . . Ma . . . seems to think that it just might be you might not have to leave at all," Brad said.

"Eh?" Dan Tackett said, leaning over the table.

"Ma"—Brad took a deep breath—"Ma seems to think that there might be a place for you and a place for the flood wall too."

The old man pulled his head back.

"Guess it might be too late, now," he said. "I reckon I have made up my mind. I don't want sympathy from the people in town. My job is finished. And I reckon that's that."

Brad swallowed hard. It had taken a lot of nerve to mention what he had just said to Dan Tackett, and it had done no good, no good at all. For a minute, he even felt mad at the old man. Brad was at least trying. Dan Tackett was not trying at all. Maybe his mother had been right. Dan Tackett was a stubborn old man. He wasn't giving the flood wall a chance. He hadn't even stopped to think about it. He was only seeing one side. But then, Brad thought suddenly, he was just like Dan Tackett. He too had looked at only one side. Neither of them had searched for an answer. They had judged the flood wall without even knowing about it.

Chapter 14

Two days passed. And to the great joy of Brad, Dan Tackett still remained on the earth, living in the small cabin against the hill. There were even times now that Brad had the feeling that the old man might not be leaving at all.

Brad thought that maybe he had been granted time to find a place for the old man. But Brad found nothing, and even his mother spoke of it no more. It seemed as if everything was waiting on him alone.

Once he had even thought of going to the flood wall and asking Mr. Hart if he might have a job for Dan Tackett. Maybe he could ask without going to the flood wall. Mr. Hart came more often than ever to his home to visit with them. He was a friendly man, Brad thought, even if he was the man who had moved Dan Tackett. More than once, he had asked Brad to come visit with him. He felt Brad would be interested in what happened to the river. It would be no time at all, he said, before the flood wall was built.

But nothing seemed to offer a solution. In the first place, if he were to go to the flood wall and find a job for the old man, he knew that Dan Tackett would not accept it. Yet Brad thought that if he could go by himself to the flood wall, he could think and observe. Maybe he could see a place where the old man was needed. But going to the flood wall would take time. If he were really to look and observe, he would have to spend almost a day. And he was afraid to leave the old man for so long a time.

This morning even Dan Tackett seemed a little surprised to be on the porch to speak as Brad walked into the yard. He looked at Brad with a sheepish look. It seemed that things had not gone as he had planned.

"Don't know what's taking so long," he said to Brad, looking up toward the clouds.

A light sprinkle of rain pattered on the leaves of the oaks, then ended just as fast as it started.

Dan Tackett sat down in the chair and stared at Brad, a frown on his face. "I reckon the time has come when you must be judged as a riverman."

Brad looked at the old man, his eyes wide.

"As you know, I have traveled to the river for my last time," Dan Tackett said. "But I have just got to know what has happened. There has been a hard rain upriver. I can tell by the clouds. They have been passing over here and going upriver for the last few days. They were heavy with rain and they could not have traveled far carrying such a load. We must know how the sand bar is setting in the river." The old man rubbed his chin. "Captain Bozer is due out of the river sometime tomorrow before daylight. If the rain above has been hard and more comes here, the river will be covered with a blanket of fog. Captain Bozer may need the light from the lantern. I have a feeling that the sand bar has built up. I can just feel it in these old bones. Funny, but in the last few years I can almost feel that river. Reckon it is because I lived on it for so long. And I got a feeling now that it is up to something. Since I cannot go to it, I reckon you will have to be my eyes."

Brad felt proud at the thought of going back to the river to judge it just as the old man had done all of these years. His heart beat fast. Then doubt swept through his mind. He had always listened close to Dan Tackett along the river, but had he listened close enough?

"Do you think you can do it?" Dan Tackett asked.

Brad looked straight into the eyes of the old man.

"Yes sir," he said. "Reckon as how I can."

"Good," Dan Tackett said. "It is a powerful lot you will have to do. Listen!"

Dan Tackett squatted to his knees and cupped his hands in front of him.

"First," he said, "you must look at the river close. Try to see if there is any brush on top of the surface. If there should be, then we will know that there has been enough swift water upriver to knock it loose from the banks. And the river will be carrying a lot of sand and mud. Look at the color of the water. Go all the way to the edge of it an stick your hand into it. Feel for a current under the surface. If there is the least current, you will feel it this way. And then too, look at the leaf of the willow. If it is hanging low, drooping, we will most likely have more rain soon." The old man squinted his eyes and studied. "Keep your ears keen to all that you hear. Watch the birds along the bank so that you can tell me what they are doing. A bird is quick to find shelter."

Brad had already gotten to his feet and stood in the yard waiting to go.

"And one more thing, Brad," Dan Tackett said. "See first of all if there is a willow left standing to hang a lantern on. And if the old willow in the yard where the cabin used to be is there, see if Cindy is still sleeping in the forks."

Brad watched the wind blow the old man's hair, and he looked at the wrinkled face and thought of the bark on the old willow tree. He waved at Dan Tackett and walked quickly through the yard.

He turned once more. Dan Tackett had sat back down in the chair, rubbing his hands together.

Chapter 15

As Brad crossed the streets of town, the thought of the river kept running over and over in his mind. He repeated again and again the many things that Dan Tackett had asked him to do. He tried to picture in his mind the river, the willows, and the birds. He had a sudden feeling that he would not be able to judge the great river. Maybe with Dan Tackett there he could, but with the old man sitting back at the cabin, Brad seemed to lose all the confidence he had ever had.

Then he thought of Captain Bozer. Captain Bozer would be depending on what Brad's eyes were able to see at the river. Once he had said that he reckoned he would have to depend on Brad to watch the river for him. He had only been joking, but it had come true. It was true enough that all he saw today would be judged by Dan Tackett when he returned to the cabin. Dan Tackett would make the final decision. But for the first time, the old man would be depending on the eyes of another for a decision.

If Dan Tackett had been right when he said there had been a rain upriver, Brad knew that the river was apt to be muddy. It would be hard to judge its rightful color. If the banks had been scraped bare, then he could not judge the leaves of the willows or the birds either. He could see the sand bar. This he could do no matter how muddy the water was. But he could not judge the depth of the water around it. And he would have to know this if he was to know how much the sand bar had built up. The wind that had come to the valley for the last few days would wrinkle the surface of the water. And if the surface of the water was wrinkled, it would be hard to tell where the shallows lay.

Brad reached the last row of brick buildings. He stopped for breath, looked toward the rim of the river bank, and a smile came to his face. He saw the top of the giant willow waving in the river wind. So far luck was with him. There at least was a place to hang the lantern.

He stood on the top of the bank staring down river, and then he scanned the sky and started to step over the edge of the bank onto the path that led where the cabin once stood.

"Hello, Brad." Brad heard the voice above the hum of the wind through the willows.

He froze in his tracks. And slowly he turned to face the tall, dark-haired man.

"Hello," Brad said.

"You know, Brad," Mr. Hart said, walking toward him, "for some time now I have had the feeling that you might be trying to dodge me. Is there any reason you know why I should feel this way?"

"I . . .I don't know," Brad said. The question had come too fast.

"Could it be something between me and your great friend, Dan Tackett?" Mr. Hart asked.

"Maybe," Brad said.

"And how is Dan Tackett getting along?" Mr. Hart asked, looking straight at Brad.

"Dan Tackett is lonely," Brad said. "You have taken the river from him."

"Did Dan Tackett tell you himself?" Mr. Hart asked.

"I . . . reckon I saw you," Brad said.

"But isn't that river still over there?" Mr. Hart pointed his finger over the bank. "You see I have not taken the river at all."

"But Dan Tackett is not here with it," Brad said.

"The river is not a long walk from where he now lives," Mr. Hart said. "And the river is free to all, I figure. I am surprised that a great riverman like Dan Tackett would not have come back to it by this time." Mr. Hart looked toward the black clouds that had formed thicker than ever along the river. "If he were here now I reckon I could sure use his advice. Building a flood wall and judging the river are two different things. The sky shows signs of bad weather. I sure would hate for the river to rise up and catch my equipment. High water right now would surely cost us a lot of time."

Brad's eyes grew wide, and he studied the words of Mr. Hart. What he said had a lot of meaning, especially since Mr. Hart also might need the judgment of Dan Tackett, who could judge the river almost to the inch.

"I suppose though," Mr. Hart said, "I am just inclined to worry over nothing at all. I have been assured that the river is not apt to rise over the banks in May. Even your mother says so, and she is a remarkable woman. I have learned to respect her judgment. But I suppose I would be more sure having the word from a great riverman like Dan Tackett."

"Anyone knows that the river is not apt to come over the banks in May," Brad said.

"I suppose anyone but me," Mr. Hart said, grinning. "I haven't been here nearly long enough to know the river that well. I have a feeling though, that I would like very much to. Catlettsburg is a friendly town. People here are mighty friendly. I have made great friends already with them all. Well . . . I should say almost all anyway."

Brad watched Mr. Hart stare straight at him, and he turned his head away.

"By the way, Brad," he asked, "what brings you

here?"

"I just came to look at the river," Brad said.

"Well," Mr. Hart said, "I am glad you came. There are a lot of things you should see."

Brad looked again at the sky above him, and a frown came to his face again. But as he stared at the black clouds, he began to think. He did have time left before dark. He heard the hum of the motors from the trucks and bulldozers upriver. His heart was beating fast, the same as it had the day he had first seen one of the giant trucks on the streets in town.

Tom Hart stood waiting.

Maybe, Brad thought, this was the chance he had been waiting for. He asked himself, how could he ever hope to help Dan Tackett if he knew nothing of the flood wall that had driven the old man from the river? If he looked at it, he might find an answer. Going with Mr. Hart would not be a complete waste of time. While he was with him, pretending to look at the flood wall, he could really be judging the river. He might learn further of Mr. Hart's plans. This way, he might have much more to tell Dan Tackett when he returned to his cabin than just the looks of the river bank and the river. He would know more than just the color of the water.

"Come with me upriver, Brad," Mr. Hart said. "Let me show you what has already been done for the good

of your town."

He turned to go and then glanced back to see if Brad was behind him.

The giant bulldozers were hard at work. And sure enough, Brad thought as he stared at them, it was a sight to see how much dirt was scooped up in one push. The high dirt wall was already beginning to take shape. It stretched along the top of the river bank like a small mountain that had been placed there and leveled on top. And over the fresh dirt, straw had been spread.

Mr. Hart placed his hand on Brad's shoulder and led him up the side of the steep wall. On top of the flood wall, Mr. Hart stopped and looked out across the river. Brad squinted his eyes.

It was a beautiful sight, Brad thought, taking a deep breath. It was like climbing to the top of a willow and scanning the river.

"Isn't it a wonderful thing, Brad?" Mr. Hart said. "I mean that men can build a flood wall and still not interfere with the real beauty of the river. Just think, with the wall in place, the town will have no more fear that the rising river might take away their homes. The town can grow, and with it will come many more new things and people. A person can plan for the future without worry of a flooded river destroying everything. Tell me . . . did you ever see such a sight?"

"Yes," Brad said, glancing along the flood wall.

"From this high up?" Mr. Hart asked.

"Reckon higher than this," Brad said.

"How?" Mr. Hart asked, squinting at Brad.

"From the top of a willow tree," Brad said.

Mr. Hart laughed and dusted his hat against the side of his leg.

"I suppose you have at that," he said, grinning. "But not everyone can climb to the top of a willow tree." Mr. Hart pointed down at the straw that covered the earth. "Later, when the flood wall is complete, we will build walks up the side of it here and there so many people can walk right up to the top with no trouble at all."

Brad watched a bulldozer swing close to the side of the wall and level the earth in front of him. The short, squatty driver looked up at him and grinned. The earth rolled in front of the large blade as if it were no heavier than a willow leaf. There was no doubt, Brad thought, the bulldozer was a great thing to see.

"Later on, Brad," Mr. Hart said, "grass will grow along the wall. There will be no naked earth left here. And the wall will add its beauty to the town. It will not be just any ordinary grass we will plant here. It will be grass to make hay. And during the summer the farmers will come and cut it and store it for winter feed for their cattle. And it will cost them nothing. We get the grass cut, and they get the hay. So you see, a flood wall can serve many purposes."

There was so much to see that Brad knew he could not possibly see it all here today. The great trucks and bulldozers rolled along the river bank, grinding and grinding.

A gust of wind swept along the top of the wall, and Brad thought again of Dan Tackett. He knew that he had wasted a lot of time. And what would the old man say if he knew that Brad was standing right now on top of the flood wall? Brad turned his head and glanced upriver. All the bank had been scraped clean except for one giant willow. It looked out of place and lonely standing on the naked lane. He tried to think why the tree had been left to stand there. Mr. Hart saw him stare.

"Curious about the willow?" he asked.

Brad stared at the willow and nodded his head.

"Well," Mr. Hart said, "let's take a look at it. I can show you better than I can tell you about it."

Brad walked up the flood wall behind Mr. Hart, now and then looking back down river toward the sand bar. This height would be a wonderful place from which to judge it. But the wall was still too far upriver. The distance was too great.

Brad and Tom Hart stopped in front of the willow. On top of the wall they were so high that they could look into the forks of the tree. Mr. Hart pointed his finger at the forks and said:

"Look there, Brad." A smile came to his face.

Brad looked into the forks and his eyes opened wide.

"What kind of birds are they, Brad?" Mr. Hart asked.

"Most anyone would know they are catbirds," Brad said surprised.

The nest of the catbird had been built of leaves and mud that had hung in the forks during the high water last year. But the outside of the nest showed signs that the bird had taken advantage of the flood wall. Yellow straw that she had gathered from the wall was woven around the outside of the nest. And loose ends here and there blew in the wind.

The mother bird was on the nest. She sat tight, her wings outstretched. From under the wings, the heads of three small birds stuck out.

"I suppose you are right," Mr. Hart said. "Most anyone would have known they were catbirds. But as I have said before, I do not know the river so well. I do know though that it would be better if we didn't stay too long. We do not want to frighten the bird. We have left the tree here for her to use until her brood is strong enough to fly. I suppose it slowed up work a little, but we weren't in that much of a hurry."

Brad walked away from the willow, back down the flood wall.

He could not understand the black-haired man that had come to Catlettsburg to build a flood wall. He had moved the home of Dan Tackett, yet he had allowed a willow tree to stand in his way, so that a bird could use it as her home. Why hadn't he felt the same way about Dan Tackett? What a wonderful thing this would have been if he had. He squinted his eyes at Mr. Hart.

"I would like to ask you a question," he said, his face turning red.

"Good," Mr. Hart said. "I was hoping that you might have many to ask."

"Why?" Brad asked. "Why would you let the catbird stay in its home in the forks of the willow tree and make Dan Tackett move from his home along the river bank?"

Mr. Hart stopped. He knelt down on one knee and picked up one of the yellow straws.

"I am glad you asked that question, Brad," Mr. Hart said. "You remember I said that I had made many friends in Catlettsburg. Well, I have. All but about two, I figure. One of them is the greatest riverman that ever came to this river. And the other is one who may some-day take his place. I have not gained their friendship be-cause they have not given me a chance. I need their friendship very much, and the town needs it too." Mr.

Hart fumbled with the straw. "I did not move the willow because the catbird is helpless with its young. Its brood is too young yet to fly, and if I destroyed the tree, they would die. Now, I moved Dan Tackett because I had to. The flood wall cannot be built any lower on the bank than it is now and no higher without taking much more of the town. Dan Tackett knew this. He could have moved himself. He was not helpless like the bird. Once the small birds have gained their flying wings, they will fly along the river until they come to a tree that will not have to be cut, and there they will make their home. They will not stay here along the flood wall pouting about the willows that I have had to cut. They will not turn away from the river just because a few trees have been cut. I had hoped that Dan Tackett would do the same. I had hoped that maybe he would search for a way that he could help the town just as much as he had in the past."

"But," Brad said, "there is nothing Dan Tackett can do but judge the river. That is his job."

"Maybe," Mr. Hart said. "But tell me, Brad, has he looked for any other way?"

Brad stared at Mr. Hart but did not answer.

"Well," Mr. Hart said, "you do not have to answer me right now. But perhaps you can think about it. I want you to know that I have great respect for Dan

Tackett. He is a wise old man, much wiser than me. He is a little stubborn, maybe, but he is too wise not to find an answer that will bring him back to his river."

Brad stared straight at Mr. Hart. Maybe in many ways his mother had been right about Mr. Hart, Brad thought. He was a kind man. If he had not been, he surely would have scraped the lone willow from the earth. He had even said that he hoped that Dan Tackett could return to the river. Had Dan Tackett been wrong? Brad put the thought away. Dan Tackett had never been wrong as far as Brad ever knew, except maybe about the automobile.

But the words of Mr. Hart kept going through his mind. Maybe the old man would return to the river. Maybe there was a job left for him. Maybe his mother was right. There just might be a place for the flood wall and Dan Tackett. If this were true, Brad thought, he would be the happiest person in the world.

"Could . . . could you maybe think of a job Dan Tackett could do?" Brad said, lowering his head.

"I surely wish I could, Brad," Mr. Hart answered. "I can build a flood wall, I suppose, but I cannot change the mind of an old man. I am afraid a man like Dan Tackett might never be satisfied unless he found the job himself."

"But . . . but how will he ever find it?" Brad asked.

"Only time will tell us, I suppose," Mr. Hart said. "One thing is sure. He will not find it by staying away from the river."

"But he is never coming back," Brad said. "He has looked at the river for the last time. He told me so."

"You know, Brad," Mr. Hart said, "years and changes can take a great deal of keenness from the eyes of an old man. Sometimes it takes his eyes a little longer to adjust to things. Maybe you can help Dan Tackett. Next to his own eyes, I believe he would trust yours."

"But how can I help him?" Brad asked.

"Why don't you try studying about the flood wall?" Mr. Hart said. "And why don't you tell him exactly what you see? Not just what you want to see."

Brad looked away and squinted his eyes down river. There was one thing now he knew for sure. He could keep his promise to his mother. He would try his best to see the good that the flood wall might bring. In fact, he felt already that it did not seem as bad as it had at first. Maybe it would really be a great thing. If there was a place for Dan Tackett, too, it would be. Now if Brad could only find a job for Dan Tackett.

But as he looked down the river, he realized that he had waited too long on top of the flood wall. Darkness would soon come to the river. Dan Tackett was waiting for him. And somewhere, coming down river now, would be Captain Bozer. He would soon be coming to the mouth of the river past the sand bar. Although Captain Bozer did not know it, he was depending on Brad. And Brad knew that he must not let him down.

"Come again tomorrow if you can," Mr. Hart said. "That is, if the rain does not come too hard for us to work." He glanced toward the sky. "We can talk some more, maybe."

So much time had passed, Brad thought. Now he tried to tell himself how he could make up for it. But you cannot make up time once it is gone.

At the edge of the river, he stopped and stuck his hand into the water. And while he held it there, he glanced across the rippled surface and tried to judge the sand bar. Pieces of brush dotted the river in places, bobbing up and down on the water. And he could feel a current. And the current was pulling toward the Kentucky shore. This, he knew, could mean that the sand carried now by the muddy water was being dropped along the edge of the sand bar, building it up and making the channel narrow. The sand could drop fast and the bar could build up in a few hours. He looked at the leaves on the willow where the joeboat was tied. The leaves drooped low. There was not a sound in the trees, except now and then a bird lost its footing and glided from one of the limbs of the willows. From everywhere was the sign of rain. And the rain would bring fog.

He wasted no time going up the bank and crossing the town to Dan Tackett's cabin. And from a distance he could see the old man pacing back and forth on the porch.

The old man listened close while Brad told of what he had seen.

"Is that all, Brad?" he asked, just as a few drops of rain fell through the trees.

Brad nodded.

The old man brought a lantern out of the cabin.

"The lantern must be hung in the willow," Dan Tackett said.

"You mean," Brad said, his eyes getting wide, "that you have to go back to the river?"

The old man shook his head.

"Now listen close, Brad," he said. "There is no doubt about it, the sand bar has built up and the channel is very narrow. Captain Bozer will have to swing the tug close to the Kentucky shore. He will be coming through a heavy fog. He will need the light so he will know to swing away from the bar. And this trip I reckon it is up to you to see that the light is in the willow."

Brad frowned. He had thought for a minute that Dan Tackett was going to return to the river. Once there, he might have found a way he could have remained with it.

The old man saw the frown on Brad's face.

"Do you think you can do it, Brad?" he asked.

Brad swallowed hard. Hanging the lantern was the truest way of all for saying that he was a real riverman.

Dan Tackett had never trusted anyone else to do it before this.

Brad shook his head and wiped the rain from his face.

"Now remember," Dan Tackett said, "shinny the willow to the first fork and hang the lantern out on the limb far enough so that the leaves won't hide the light. Captain Bozer will be looking for it. He must know that the channel is narrow."

The old man fumbled in his pocket. He pulled out a shiny piece of tinfoil.

"Here are matches," he said. "The tinfoil will keep them dry. You will have to hurry to beat the rain that is coming. It will be too late for you to come back to the cabin after you have hung the lantern. Now hurry, Brad. And mind the willow. The bark will be as slick as the skin of a catfish."

Brad took the lantern and started out of the yard.

"Don't forget," Dan Tackett hollered, "pull the globe down on the lantern. If you don't the wind and rain will put out the light."

Chapter 16

The lantern swung back and forth in Brad's hand as he hurried out of the yard. He listened to the kerosene sloshing back and forth in the container on the bottom of the lantern, and fearing that it might somehow get out of the metal container, he pulled the lantern to his chest and carried it.

He did not stop until he came to the last row of brick buildings. And here he rested for a minute, for he knew that climbing the giant willow would take wind and strength.

At the edge of the building, he glanced toward the river; it was only a few more steps away now. Dan Tackett had been right; the fog had moved in quickly, and as if it had been beat low to the earth by the rain, it hovered over the river.

Brad watched the fog drift through the tops of the willows like great puffs of gray smoke.

He hurried to the giant willow. Here under the willow, he stopped long enough to loop the handle of the lantern through his belt. He would need both hands to climb the tree. He felt again to make sure that the matches were still in his pocket. Then he took a deep breath and started up the trunk of the tree.

The bark was slick. But here and there along the trunk the old bark had peeled leaving small footholds for him to use. He reached his hand toward the first fork, and grabbing into the center of it, he pulled himself into it. From higher in the tree, he heard the catbird, Cindy, quarrel and talk to her brood that was hidden under her wings. She knew that someone was in the tree. But Brad knew that she would sit tight to the nest, protecting her brood.

Standing in the fork of the tree, he reached over toward a limb where he might hang the lantern. He hung the lantern on a stub, and then waited to see if it would hold there in the wind. But now he could not hold the globe and cup a hand over the match to keep the wind from blowing it out at the same time. He would have to shinny out on the limb.

The limb swung down under his weight. He drew in a deep breath and stopped. For a moment, he was afraid the limb might break, but then he remembered what Dan Tackett had told him about the willow. In May the sap is in the tree and the limbs will bend to the ground before they will break. He took another deep breath and climbed out on the limb so that he could reach the lantern.

He lifted the globe carefully and, cupping a match

from the wind, lit the small wick under the globe. Then he hurried back down the limb to the fork of the tree. The light flickered, burst into a flame and then swayed under the wind and went out. He squinted his eyes. He had forgotten to close the globe.

Back out to the limb he crawled. This time he lit the wick, closed the globe, and stayed on the swaying limb until he was sure it was burning. When the flame grew bright, he climbed out of the tree.

On the top of the bank, he stopped and looked back at the light, his chest swelling with pride. His pants were soaked through from climbing the wet tree, and he knew that he would have to hurry home.

Brad knew that his mother would be pacing the floor, waiting for him. So he took a last look and hurried across town. What would Captain Bozer think, he wondered, when he found out that it had been Brad who had lit the lantern this trip? He would surely be surprised to learn that it had been Brad who had guided his way. Maybe now he would not bother to blow a long and a short blast of his whistle. Maybe there would be two long blasts.

During the night, the rain came heavily. It beat against the window so hard that Brad could not sleep. Every time he closed his eyes, he thought he could see the light from the lantern flicker and go out. And once when he fell asleep, he dreamed that he had forgotten to close the globe. He had returned to the river at daylight to see the small tug lodged on the sand bar. In his dream, just the front part of the hull was all that he had been able to see. The rest of the boat was under water. He searched the river bank for signs of Captain Bozer, but he too was gone. He woke from the dream and lay awake.

It was not an easy job to judge the great river, he thought. Maybe he had not been able to see the things that really counted. Maybe Dan Tackett had not been able to tell from what Brad had seen. Even now there was no way to be sure that the light would stay lit. Dan Tackett had been there in the cabin beside the lantern all night, and he could look any time he wanted to and see the light.

Brad tried to remember if he had done exactly as Dan Tackett had told him to do. And once during the night, he thought he would get up and travel back to the river and stay there until Captain Bozer came by. But his mother would know that he had left the house. Sometimes, Brad thought, she had ears as keen as the ears of the kingfisher. She had a way of knowing things. He could only wait for daylight.

Chapter 17

Daylight finally came, and Brad was up to meet it. The rain still dripped from the roof of the house, and the air was still and heavy with fog.

Brad dressed and sneaked through the house as quietly as he could. With luck, he was thinking, he could sneak to the river and be back to the house before his mother was up and missed him. He could bring the lantern to his house, eat breakfast, and then take the lantern back to the cabin of Dan Tackett.

He tiptoed past her door. And as he passed it, he noticed that it had been left partly open during the night. He hurried past it to the front door.

"Brad." He heard his mother's voice, and he froze in his tracks. "Be careful, and as quick as you fetch the lantern from the willow tree come back to the house for your breakfast."

Brad walked out the door. There was one thing for sure, he thought as he hurried through the yard; he would never try to fool his mother again. He wondered how she could know so much.

The closer to the river he got, the faster he walked. He would soon be close enough to see the light hanging in the tree.

So early in the morning the streets were deserted and lonely.

Brad stopped at the corner of one of the brick buildings and squinted his eyes toward the top of the river bank. There was no light to be seen!

From down on the river bank, he heard a murmur of voices. Over these voices came a deeper one, it sounded as if it came from out in the river.

"Dan Tackett!" The deep voice rolled up the river bank. "Dan Tackett!"

And Brad knew the voice. It was Captain Bozer.

Brad ran to the river bank. He passed under the giant willow, stopping long enough to look up through the limbs. The lantern still hung from the stub, swinging back and forth in the wind. But there was no globe in the lantern. He could see a limb hanging against the lantern. He looked quickly to the ground under the willow. Glass was scattered everywhere. The dead limb had fallen and broken the globe and the wind had snuffed out the flame.

Brad ran on down the river bank. He saw men standing there, moving quickly about and looking over the surface of the river toward the sand bar.

"Dan Tackett!" Captain Bozer's voice came again across the water.

Brad tried to see across the water. He could just make out the small tug, against the sand bar, leaning on one side. The boat had run aground. Brad knew now what had happened. Captain Bozer had come down the river in the fog and, seeing no light, he had guessed that the channel was clear. He had not bothered to steer close to the Kentucky shore line, and he had hit the sand bar.

As Brad came closer to the men at the edge of the river, he saw that one of them was Mr. Hart, and another was the bulldozer operator. Several other men had gathered nearby.

Now that he was close to the river, Brad could make out the figure of Captain Bozer. Brad watched the big man run to one side of the boat. He hollered again for Dan Tackett. As he moved the small tug tilted back and forth.

Mr. Hart turned and looked toward Brad.

"Lucky I came early this morning to see what the rain did to the river during the night," he said.

Tears filled Brad's eyes.

"Captain Bozer will sink," he said. "I know he will sink. He will not be able to make if off the bar."

"It does look mighty bad," Mr. Hart said, squinting his eyes as he looked across the water. "We have got to think fast."

Mr. Hart rubbed his chin. His eyes came to rest on

Dan Tackett's small joeboat.

"I wonder," he said, still rubbing his chin. "I wonder if the water is deep enough to pull the joeboat to the side of the tug out there. What do you think, Brad?"

Brad strained his eyes, trying the best he could to judge the depth of the river. The river was muddy and the fog moved over it slowly. He made out the outline of the bar. He tried to remember the many things that Dan Tackett had taught him about the river. He tried to remember all the ways in which he was to judge the sand bar. But he could not think clearly. In fact, it seemed that he had forgotten all the old man had ever taught him about the river.

"I . . . I don't know," Brad said, wiping his eyes and looking across the surface of the river again.

"Well," Mr. Hart said, "it seems to me that this is the only way we will ever be able to help that man out there. That is, if we can help him at all."

"Captain Bozer will sink," Brad said, wiping his eyes again. He glanced toward the joeboat.

"Captain Bozer, did you say?" Mr. Hart asked. "Is that the name of the man who is out there on the small boat?"

"Yes," Brad said.

"Captain Bozer!" Mr. Hart hollered across the water.

"That you, Dan Tackett?" the voice came back across

the water.

"No!" Mr. Hart answered. "It is not Dan Tackett. Can you swim?"

"Sure!" Captain Bozer yelled back.

"You are closer to the other bank!" Mr. Hart yelled. "Can you make it from where you are?"

The river became quiet for a minute.

"Not without my boat!" Captain Bozer said.

"This is no time to be funny," Mr. Hart said to himself, shaking his head.

"If the boat stays, I stay!" Captain Bozer bellowed.

Mr. Hart shook his head again.

"I am beginning to believe," he said, to nobody in particular, "that these rivermen are the stubbornest people I have ever met."

"Dan Tackett!" Captain Bozer yelled again. "Where are you? Brad! Are you there?"

"Captain Bozer!" Brad yelled, walking as close to the edge of the river as he could.

"That you, Brad?" Captain Bozer said.

"Yes!" Brad answered.

"Brad," the voice came back, "git Dan Tackett! Blast his hide!"

"Dan Tackett is not here!" Brad answered.

"Then go fetch him! And hurry! I am taking water!"

Brad looked at Mr. Hart. And Mr. Hart looked away

and motioned to the bulldozer man a short way up the bank from him. The man walked toward him.

"Go upriver," Mr. Hart said, "and bring the bulldozer. Get enough cable from one of the trucks to reach from here to the boat on the sand bar."

"How are you planning to get the cable out to the boat?" the man asked.

"Never mind right now," Mr. Hart said. "Just you get the bulldozer and cable here as fast as you can." Mr. Hart turned and stared at Brad. "So you are not sure about the depth of the river, eh?"

Brad shook his head.

"Well," Mr. Hart said, "there is only one person I know who will be sure. Dan Tackett. You must hurry to his cabin, Brad. Go as quickly as you can. Bring Dan Tackett back to the river. This is our only chance."

"But what if Dan Tackett won't come back to the river?" Brad asked.

Mr. Hart rubbed his chin.

"I believe he will come," Mr. Hart said. "He is a stubborn old man all right. But he is also a riverman, and that is a riverman out there. Rivermen stick together as close as willows to the river."

Chapter 18

"Dan Tackett! Dan Tackett!" Brad hollered as he ran through the yard onto the porch of the small cabin. He pounded on the front door.

The door opened and the old man looked down at Brad.

"What is it, Brad?" he asked. "Here now, catch your breath and tell me."

"You have got to come to the river," Brad said. "And you have got to hurry, Dan Tackett. Mr. Hart says that you don't have a minute to lose."

Dan Tackett brushed the hair out of his eyes and stooped to tie one of his shoes. And then he straightened up and stared at Brad.

"He does, does he?" Dan Tackett said. "Well, you can go back to the river and tell this Mr. Hart that there ain't no flood wall man telling me what to do!"

"But . . . " Brad frowned and stared back toward the river. "You have just got to come, Dan Tackett." Brad caught his breath.

"Now, what's this?" Dan Tackett said.

"It ain't altogether Mr. Hart," Brad said. "Mostly it's Captain Bozer!" Brad wiped tears from his eyes.

"Eh?" Dan Tackett said, bending his ear toward Brad. "What's Captain Bozer got to do with it all?"

"He is grounded on top of the sand bar!" Brad said. "A limb fell from the top of the willow during the storm and broke the globe of the lantern, and the light went out. Hurry, please, Dan Tackett. Captain Bozer is going to sink. He wouldn't leave the boat like Mr. Hart asked him to do."

"The old fool," Dan Tackett said, frowning. "He's traveled up and down that river a thousand times in weather worse than this, and the first time I turn my back, he runs aground. I ought to just let him sink!"

Just the same, the old man stepped from the porch and hurried out of the yard with Brad. He limped across town so fast that it was hard for Brad to keep up with him. On top of the bank, he stopped and looked around. He eyed the giant willow, still standing on the shore. And he rubbed his chin as if he were surprised. In fact, the whole river bank here at the mouth of the river looked the same. It had not been touched so far.

"Dan Tackett!" Captain Bozer's voice drifted across the river just as the old man reached the edge of the water.

Dan Tackett quickly stooped and stuck his hand into the river. He squinted his eyes and looked around him, at the trees and then at the sand bar.

"Ain't no use yelling," Dan Tackett hollered. "Ain't no use to wake up the town just 'cause you got a little sand under that tug."

"Wouldn't of been there if you hadn't gone traipsing off!" Captain Bozer yelled back. "Now you get me off of here. I am taking water fast!"

Dan Tackett looked around him. He cocked his ear as the sound of a motor came over the river. He turned and watched a giant bulldozer come down the bank and stop in front of him. The man in the bulldozer jumped out and pulled the end of the cable from a large spool that he had fastened on the back of the bulldozer. He nodded his head to Mr. Hart and then looked again over the river toward the sand bar.

"Stay on the high side of the boat, Bozer!" Dan Tackett cupped his hand and yelled across the water. "Quit jumping around out there!"

"You get me and my boat to shore, Dan Tackett!" Captain Bozer yelled.

"Is the water in the river deep enough to take the joeboat out to the tug?" Mr. Hart spoke for the first time, looking straight at Dan Tackett.

Dan Tackett looked around and a frown came to his face. He brushed the hair from his eyes.

"I am not talking about the flood wall now, Dan Tackett," Mr. Hart said. "I am asking your judgment.

Can the joeboat make it out there? If it can't, Captain Bozer and the tug are going down."

Brad stood staring at the old man. Dan Tackett squinted his eyes and stared out over the river. He stomped his feet, patting holes in the soft sand.

"Maybe," he said, studying the water again. "Depends."

"Depends on what?" Mr. Hart asked.

"Depends who is in the joeboat," Dan Tackett said. "And how well the man that is in the joeboat knows the river. There might just be a channel deep enough to make it. But you would have to know the channel and how to handle a small boat in a current."

"All right," Mr. Hart said. "That is all I wanted to know. I have a plan, Dan Tackett. I figure that if you can take the loose end of this cable on the bulldozer out to the tug, I can pull the boat to shore with my tractor. What do you say?"

Dan Tackett studied the river again. He kicked around in the sand again with his shoes. And then he looked at Mr. Hart and squinted his eyes.

"I ain't working with no flood wall man," he said. "Don't seem to me you had trouble getting to my cabin when it was on the river bank. Now, let's see you take the bulldozer out to the tug." The old man folded his arms.

Tears welled deep in Brad's eyes.

"It was my fault, Dan Tackett," Brad said. "I hung the lantern. And now Captain Bozer will sink. And it will be my fault!" Brad wiped his eyes again.

"Now, Brad," Dan Tackett said, putting his hand on Brad's shoulder. "Ain't no fault of yours because the dead limb fell from the tree."

"Well!" Mr. Hart said, looking at Dan Tackett. "You can spite me all you want, but Bozer will sink just the same."

Dan Tackett turned his head quickly. He frowned at Mr. Hart.

"And what makes you so sure that you could pull the boat off the sand bar even if I could take the cable out there?" Dan Tackett asked.

"And what makes you so sure that you can take the cable out there even if I can pull the boat off with my tractor?" Mr. Hart asked back.

"Listen, young man!" Dan Tackett said, setting his feet solid in the sand. "I been following the channels of this river before you were born, and in lots worse times than this, too. You pay mind to your new-fangled machinery, and I'll pay mind and take my chances with this river. Now, when I get in the joeboat, Brad, you hand me the end of that cable."

The old man untied the boat, stepped into it and

pulled a set of oars from the floor of the boat and put them in the oarlocks on the sides of it. He took the end of the cable and fastened it to the back of the joeboat. The old man took an oar and pushed it to the bottom of the water and shoved off.

The old man quickly straightened the joeboat against the current and pulled slowly across the river. The wind was keen, and it blew his hair back and forth in his eyes. But now the old man could not let go of the oars long enough to brush the hair away. Instead he jerked his head back and forth. He allowed the boat to drift with the current, not trying to fight it. But all the time, he was pulling farther out in the river. He would drift down river, farther than the sand bar. Once even with the sand bar, the current would be broken, and he would row straight upriver toward the point of the bar.

Now people had gathered on the bank, and they all watched the old man. Mr. Hart strained to guide the cable, keeping it loose so that it would not tighten and pull against Dan Tackett. Now and then the old man pulled an oar out of the locks and stuck it over the side of the boat into the river. He would push the oar up and down, and Brad knew that he was gauging the depth of the river, trying to touch the bottom to determine the shallow spots.

He reached the small tug and held the end of the oar

out for Captain Bozer to grab. Captain Bozer grabbed the oar and held the joeboat fast.

Brad could see the old man and Captain Bozer shaking their heads, but he could not hear what they were saying. Maybe Dan Tackett was telling Captain Bozer that it had been Brad who had lit the lantern. Brad felt ashamed.

The old man handed the end of the cable to Captain Bozer, and he tied it to the small tug. But he would not leave the tug. He handed the oar back to Dan Tackett and watched while the small joeboat drifted away and the old man rowed toward the shore.

"All right," Mr. Hart said to the man in the bulldozer. "Go slow until the boat is off the sand bar."

The treads of the bulldozer sank deep into the sand and turned over slowly. The cable tightened and the small tug tilted farther on its side and slid slowly from the sand bar. It nosed toward the Kentucky shore. Mr. Hart motioned toward the bulldozer. The motor purred louder and the tug moved swiftly through the current.

The small tug almost beat the joeboat to the shore and Captain Bozer stepped out onto the bank and stared at Dan Tackett.

"Just about my luck, Dan Tackett," he said, wiping his face. "My last trip upriver in this old tug and I almost lose her. Just when I got myself a fine trade-in."

"Trade-in!" Dan Tackett said.

Captain Bozer grinned. "You are looking at an old man that has gained new life. Ain't no use for us to kid each other any longer about it, Dan Tackett. The world is leaving us. We can't stay behind any longer. Me, I got my eyes set on a new boat as shiny as a new silver dollar. Lots of room to get around on her, too. Twice as big as this tug. And fast? Not a current in the river that can hold her." Captain Bozer brushed the red hair back over his head. "Yep, Dan Tackett, I can haul more store goods up this Big Sandy to trade on one trip than I can do most of the summer on this tug. The world is moving fast, I say. But you watch Bozer here. Old Captain Bozer is going to be right out there in front of the rest blowing his boat horn the loudest."

Dan Tackett looked at Captain Bozer and squinted his eyes.

"I ought to have left you out there on the sand bar," he said.

The old man walked to the willow and began to fasten his joeboat back to the limb of the tree.

Mr. Hart walked toward Captain Bozer and a smile was on his face.

"Captain Bozer," he said, reaching out his hand, "I am Tom Hart. I'm in charge of building the flood wall around Catlettsburg."

Captain Bozer reached out his large hand.

"Mighty fine bulldozer you got there," Captain Bozer said. "Reckon I owe you a heap of thanks. Flood wall, eh." Captain Bozer rubbed his chin. "Old town sure needs it bad. Never thought it would actually, build one though, I reckon."

Dan Tackett looked back toward the two men. He squinted his eyes and frowned.

"Could I help you fasten your boat to the shore?" Mr. Hart asked, pointing to the tug.

"Well, now," Captain Bozer said, "reckon that would be mighty neighborly of you indeed."

The two men walked down the bank to the tug. Brad could see them talking, but he could not hear them. Now and then they would both look toward the old man and Captain Bozer would rub his chin. And once or twice he shook his head, and then again a grin would be on his face as he watched Dan Tackett fumble with the rope that held the joeboat. Mr. Hart was talking fast, and it looked as though Captain Bozer was agreeing to every word he said.

Finally, they came back up the bank.

"River is rough, Captain Bozer," Mr. Hart said. "I suppose you will be waiting for it to settle down some." He kicked at the ground under his feet. "Ground is too wet for us to work with it today too, it looks like. I would consider it a privilege if you were to be my guest during your stay on shore."

"Well now, Tom Hart," Captain Bozer said, "I consider that kind of you indeed."

Dan Tackett wiped his face with the sleeve of his shirt. He stared for a minute at Captain Bozer, and then he straightened up and walked past them up the bank. He did not look back.

"Dan Tackett!" Brad said, and he turned to follow the old man up the bank.

But the large hand of Captain Bozer reached out and grabbed his arm. And Brad stopped in his tracks.

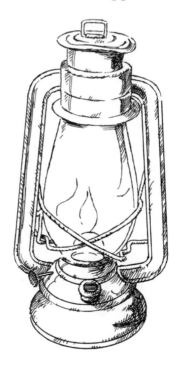

Chapter 19

The sun was low now in the sky above the valley. The rain was over and during the day a giant rainbow had come, leaned for a while against the side of the clouds, and then had disappeared from sight. The sun had made the day warm.

Slowly Brad walked down the path that followed the foot of the hills to the cabin of the old man. He was not sure that he should be going to the cabin now. He was doing it for Captain Bozer, but he wished he understood more about the message Captain Bozer had given him to carry to Dan Tackett.

As Brad walked slowly along he thought over the words of Captain Bozer. "Tell Dan Tackett that Captain Bozer wants him to come as quickly as he can," he had told Brad. "As quickly as his legs will carry him." Captain Bozer had rubbed his large hands through his hair and laughed. "If Dan Tackett don't stir in his seat," Captain Bozer had said, "lean close to him and tell him that old Bozer has got a plan concerning the flood wall."

Dan Tackett would be sure to come. Captain Bozer was as sure as he could be about it. "And, Brad, if even that don't work, tell him your ma wants to see him. That will bring him sure."

Before Brad realized it, he had reached the cabin of Dan Tackett. He squinted his eyes through the yard. The old man sat in the chair on the porch, his hands folded and his head down. His hands were hanging in front of him, and he gripped them tightly. Brad eyed the old man, took a deep breath and walked to the porch.

The old man heard him and looked up. He stared at Brad, squinting his eyes. And then a smile came to his face.

"By-doggies, Brad," he said, "is that you? I had thought that maybe you had forgotten old Dan Tackett."

Brad looked away and sat down on the edge of the porch.

"I. . .I am glad that you are still here at the cabin, Dan Tackett," Brad said. "I was afraid you might be gone before I got here."

Dan Tackett looked toward the river.

"Guess I just misjudged the amount of work the good Lord might have to do," the old man said. "Reckon too, in a way, I misjudged about everything. And about everybody, especially my old friends. All of them too, excepting maybe you, Brad. And I guess I never knew the world could be so lonely without them."

Brad watched the old man fumble with the sleeve of his shirt.

"You know something, Brad?" he said. "I have had time to sit here and think today. It just might be that this here flood wall ain't such a bad thing after all. I reckon I know that that river has been tugging at the town for a long time, taking a piece of it away each year."

Brad squinted his eyes and tried to understand what the old man had just said.

"Yes sir," Dan Tackett said, "the flood wall just might save the town after all, and it will be a good thing for you, Brad."

"But what about you, Dan Tackett?" Brad asked.

"Shucks," the old man said, "don't make much difference where I am concerned. Can't you see, Brad, my job is over. This is your world. It is not a world for an old man like me."

Brad stared at Dan Tackett.

"Guess I never was much for words," Dan Tackett said. "Never could untangle them so that I could say what I wanted to say with them. But there ought to be a way for me to tell you what I would like for you to know." He rubbed his chin.

"You remember, Brad," the old man said, "you remember that big willow that used to set down the river bank from my cabin? The one that had no leaves at all on it. The dead tree that the river washed away last year."

Brad thought for a minute of the tree and then nodded his head.

"Well," Dan Tackett said, "I remember when that tree was not nearly so big. But I knew it was one of the first trees along the river to sprout leaves in the spring. I used to watch it during the summer, standing there with its roots full of sap, holding the bank together so that the land would not slip away. It was so much bigger than the other trees around it that it almost looked to be standing alone." Dan Tackett rubbed his hands through his hair. "And then one summer there were no leaves on the limbs of this willow. The tree was old. Its job was done."

"Now what it should have done was to fall and be carried away by the river so that there would be room for another tree to take its place. But do you think it would fall? No sir. It just stood there all the same, its limbs peeling off its bark, and the flesh underneath the bark was as brown as the boards of my cabin here. It stood for a whole year trying to fool the river into thinking that it was still doing the job it was there on the river to do. It was just too stubborn to fall and make room for a younger tree. But it didn't fool the river. No sir. The river knew that the roots of the old willow were dried up and brittle. There was no longer any need for it there. So one night, the river rose up and swept it from the river bank forever."

"And the way I see it, Brad, they ain't a lot of difference between me and that old river willow. My job is over. I reckon that I was too stubborn to move. I just kept thinking that there was a job left for me, just like the willow. But the river knew better, but it would not be so easy to get rid of me. I had learned the river very well, and I was even more stubborn than that willow. I reckon it took a flood wall to move me."

"But . . . but," Brad said, squinting his eyes, "maybe there is still a job for you, Dan Tackett. Captain Bozer thinks that there is. That's why . . . why he sent me to fetch you to come back to my house where he is waiting."

Dan Tackett quickly raised his head.

"Bozer!" he said. "Bozer sent you?"

"Captain Bozer says that he's just got to see you," Brad said. "He says that you have to hurry."

"Well!" Dan Tackett said. "You can tell Captain Bozer that the river will be apt to dry up before I come. I ought to have left him out there on the sand bar!"

Brad leaned close.

"Captain Bozer says for me to tell you that he has a plan concerning the flood wall," Brad said.

Dan Tackett squinted his eyes and leaned close.

"The flood wall?" he said, rubbing his hand under

his chin.

"He says that he will be waiting for you at my house," Brad said.

"I wonder," Dan Tackett said. "Now what could that Bozer be up to? Did you see him back at the river, Brad? Took up with that Tom Hart. 'Mighty fine machinery,' he said." Dan Tackett drew up his mouth to mock Captain Bozer. "What does he know about machinery? He is a riverman just like me. Trading his boat! But then . . . it ain't like Captain Bozer to turn against me. I wonder . . . Nope. I won't do it. And you can go back and tell Bozer so."

"But . . . but Ma says that you must be sure to come," Brad said. "She has got to see you right away." Brad frowned. This was his last chance.

"Your ma said that?" Dan Tackett said.

Brad nodded his head.

"Then I must go," Dan Tackett said. "But mind you now, Brad; it is only for your mother. I don't know as I trust Captain Bozer. But your mother would not try to trick me. But, seems to me I overheard Captain Bozer making plans to be with this Tom Hart today. Are you sure there is no one at the house but your ma and Captain Bozer?"

"Yes," Brad said. "There is only the two of them."

Chapter 20

Brad followed the old man out of the yard and they walked quickly toward the house. In the front yard of Brad's house, Dan Tackett stopped and took a deep breath and pulled his pants up higher around his waist. He squinted his eyes at Brad and followed him quickly through the front door.

He squinted his eyes in the large room and stopped. He looked toward Brad.

"What . . . what is this, Brad?" he asked.

Brad's eyes grew wide. He looked around at all of the people in the room. It seemed to Brad that no more people could have crowded in. Mr. Hart sat in front of the room at a table, just as he had the first night he had come to the house. Captain Bozer sat on one side of him and on the other side sat Brad's mother. Everyone in the room was staring at Dan Tackett.

Dan Tackett looked straight at Captain Bozer.

"You have fooled me, Bozer!" he said, beginning to turn.

And I have tricked him too, Brad thought. And so has my own mother.

"Now wait," Captain Bozer said. "Wait, you old river

fool!"

Dan Tackett turned quickly to face him again.

"Please wait, Dan Tackett," Brad's mother said, rising from her chair. "The town needs you badly."

Dan Tackett squinted his eyes toward her.

"Needs . . . needs me?" he mumbled.

"Yes," Brad's mother said, smiling at Brad now. "We have always needed you, Dan Tackett. But, according to Mr. Hart, we need you now worse than ever before."

Dan Tackett stared toward Tom Hart.

"Please stay and listen," Brad's mother said. "And then if you wish to go we will not try to stop you."

Dan Tackett squinted his eyes slowly around the room, and he took a seat in a chair close to the door. He eyed Captain Bozer, and Captain Bozer looked back at him with a great smile on his face. Brad watched Captain Bozer fumble with a small cardboard box he held in his lap.

"Perhaps I can explain." Tom Hart broke the silence of the room. He took his pencil and ran it along the map on the top of the table. "Here is the problem. I did not know until this morning when I was towing Captain Bozer's boat off the sand bar that the earth in this particular section of the river bank was so soft. I looked it over very carefully today. And I know now that if I scrape off the willows that grow there and push the earth up into a high mound to form the flood wall, the dirt will slip away. There will be nothing to hold it. The earth there is just too soft. I am afraid that in a year or two the wall would slip right down into the river. The only way I can see to right this is to leave the willows standing there in the earth to hold the land together. But to do this I must change my plans. I must build a concrete wall along the top of the river bank at this point of the town. I must build it back a little farther into town than I had expected. It would take a bit more of the city. But you have all agreed to let me have this land."

Dan Tackett squinted his eyes again and watched the people in the room closely.

"But," Tom Hart said, "this is only one problem solved. There is something else I overlooked. But thanks to Captain Bozer I have caught the problem in time." He looked up at Dan Tackett. "This section of town is the main section. It is here, where the concrete wall must be built, that the town has the best access to the river. Now, I can build steps up a dirt wall and all can walk them. But I cannot build steps up the side of a steep concrete wall. I will have to build a ladder. And this will not be easy to climb. And as the town grows, so will the travel on the river"—Mr. Hart glanced at Captain Bozer again — "thanks to Captain Bozer for reminding me about this. Therefore, there must be a way where the town will have free access to the river. And this must be right where the concrete wall will be built. The only thing I can do is to build a gate in the high wall—a gate that can open when the river is low and close when the river is high. And this is the problem. There must be a sure way of knowing when the river will rise, so that the gate can be closed. We must find someone to handle the gate. Not just anyone. But it must be a man who knows the river well. He must be able to judge it. The town will be depending on the judgment of this man. And I might add that it would seem to me that whoever you choose should live as close to the river as he could. He should be there beside it to watch it."

"Well, now," Captain Bozer reared back in his chair. "What about Dan Tackett for the job? Ain't a man in Kentucky that has his knowledge of the river. In fact, he has been with the river so long, he has begun to favor it in looks."

Everyone in the room stared at Dan Tackett. The old man squirmed in his chair.

"Captain Bozer," Tom Hart said, "you ought to have been an engineer. That's a great idea. Who could possibly know the river better than Dan Tackett? And . . . why he has a house site already there, too. I could move his cabin back tomorrow. All in favor of Dan Tackett returning to the river raise your hands."

All hands in the room went high into the air. And all eyes watched Dan Tackett. The old man wiped his eyes with the sleeve of his shirt.

"Please, Dan Tackett," Brad said.

"The town really needs you, Dan Tackett," Brad's mother said.

"Reckon . . . reckon," Dan Tackett said, "if the town really needs an old man like me, I would be ready to go back home."

"Can we shake on it?" Mr. Hart said, walking across the room.

Dan Tackett reached out his hand.

"One thing, Tom Hart," Dan Tackett said. "I never thought you could pull that tug off the sand bar with that bulldozer."

Tom Hart laughed.

"You know," he said, "I never thought you could make it to the sand bar with that joeboat either."

They both laughed.

And Brad was so happy that he thought he could easily jump and touch the ceiling of the room. But there were too many people there for him to try. Everyone was up shaking hands with Dan Tackett and the old man was grinning.

"Well, then." The room grew quiet for a minute. Captain Bozer walked across the room. "Now that this is settled"—he held the box that he had kept on his lap toward Brad—"this is for you, Brad."

Brad took the box.

"Open it," Captain Bozer said.

Brad opened the box. And from it he pulled out a shiny new lantern. And it was not an ordinary lantern. It was not like the one he had hung in the willow tree. The wind would not blow this one out. Brad pushed the little switch on the side of it and a bright light blinked on. It worked by battery.

"I got it for a real bargain," Captain Bozer said. "Traded Tom Hart here for it. And I wanted you to have it, Brad. Can't tell when this Dan Tackett might take a notion to go traipsing off again." He squinted his eyes at Dan Tackett. "I sure skinned Tom Hart in the trade, too."

"What did you trade him for it?" Brad asked, fumbling with the light.

"Just three toots of my boat whistle," Captain Bozer said. "Seems that Tom Hart here has taken a notion all of a sudden to become a riverman as well as an engineer. So there will be a whistle for Dan Tackett, one for you, Brad, and one for Tom Hart."

"I suppose I will have to try to learn this river so that I can earn the whistle from the boat," Tom Hart said. "I would like to try something else too. I have been traveling on rivers all of my life, it seems, building flood walls. I have been living alone and doing my own cooking for all of these years. But I have at last come to a town where I have made friends with everyone. Now, if I thought I could find someone to cook for me, I just might decide to stay here from now on." He looked across the room at Brad's mother and Brad saw him wink. And he saw his mother blush. "But right now," Tom Hart said, "I have got a cabin to move. Are you ready, Dan Tackett?"

Dan Tackett nodded his head.

"Can I ride on the porch with Dan Tackett?" Brad asked following them out of the house.

"If you want to ride with us," Tom Hart said, "you will have to ride in the front seat."

Dan Tackett looked at Brad and grinned.

And Brad looked once again toward the rim of the town. And he remembered the words of his mother. Catlettsburg was a small town. But there was room for a flood wall. There was room for a river. And there was also room for Dan Tackett.

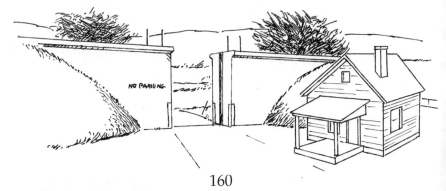